SO-CNI-615

STOP THAT TRAIN!

The locomotive ground to a halt, its cowcatcher fifty feet from the tree across the tracks. From behind the tree, Captain Gringo opened up with his Maxim, raking the train with hot lead as others with him opened up with small arms.

"Throw her in reverse!" Hernan screamed. But a slug blew him off the side of the locomotive, screaming, gut shot. Another machine gun round smashed into the engineer's forehead, spattering the fireman with blood and brains. The fireman reversed the gears and opened the throttle wide. Then a bullet went in one ear and out the other. Now nobody was at the controls as the ladrone train backed off, picking up speed with every thrust of its drivers.

The train rolled out across the trestle. As it got to the middle, the dynamite went off with a thunderous roar, lifting trestle and train, then dropping the screaming ladrones into the deep waters below!

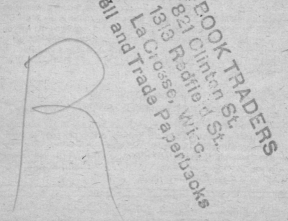
BOOK TRADERS
821 Clinton St.
1313 Redfield St.
La Crosse, Wis.
Sell and Trade Paperbacks

Novels by Ramsay Thorne

Published by
WARNER BOOKS

CALLING ALL MEN OF ACTION...

Please drop us a card with your name and address and we'll keep you up-to-date on all the great forthcoming books in our MEN OF ACTION series—you'll know in advance what is coming out so you won't miss any of these exciting adventures. We would also enjoy your comments on the books you have read. Send to: SPECIAL SALES DEPARTMENT, WARNER BOOKS, 666 FIFTH AVENUE, NEW YORK, N.Y. 10103.

**ARE THERE WARNER BOOKS
YOU WANT BUT CANNOT FIND IN YOUR LOCAL STORES?**

You can get any WARNER BOOKS title in print. Simply send title and retail price, plus 50¢ per order and 20¢ per copy to cover mailing and handling costs for each book desired. New York State and California residents add applicable sales tax. Enclose check or money order only, no cash please, to: WARNER BOOKS, P.O. BOX 690, NEW YORK, N.Y. 10019.

Renegade #16

MEXICAN MARAUDER

by
Ramsay Thorne

WARNER BOOKS

A Warner Communications Company

WARNER BOOKS EDITION

Copyright © 1983 by Lou Cameron
All rights reserved.

Warner Books, Inc.,
666 Fifth Avenue,
New York, N.Y. 10103

 A Warner Communications Company

Printed in the United States of America

First Printing: January, 1983

10 9 8 7 6 5 4 3 2 1

Renegade #16

MEXICAN MARAUDER

The orgy was going on in one wing of a Central American villa that had been fixed up to look like a Turkish harem. Ruby glass lights cast their whorehouse glow on naked ladies of diverse race and form as they lounged languidly on cushion-strewn oriental rugs, awaiting their master's next whim. In the center of the rug, Sir Basil Hakim, who owned Woodbine Arms, Ltd., as well as the villa and everyone in it, was trying to work up an erection.

It wasn't easy. Sir Basil, sometimes called the Merchant of Death, was a dirty old man who looked even older, thanks to the life he'd led. As he drooled at the bevy of beautiful, willing love slaves all around him, he was on his hands and knees, taking it in the ass from a big, well-hung Haitian sailor, while the half-dozen harem girls watched, bemused.

Neither Sir Basil nor his black lover was a true homosexual. The Haitian was embarrassed to be doing a bitty white man in the brown with ladies watching. But he was

7

desperately broke, stranded in British Honduras after jumping ship, and what the hell, there were harder ways to make this much money.

Sir Basil was a totally dedicated degenerate, but he generally preferred to be sodomizing man, woman, or beast instead of offering his derriere as the target. The jaded little pervert had been told by his doctor that he needed a daily prostate massage to restore his abused genitourinary tract, and it seemed silly to pay a medic to stick his finger up one's arse when there were naughtier ways to produce the same effect. Sir Basil knew he was shocking even his blasé mistresses with this newest perverse foreplay, and that was fun, too. His anal opening had started to relax around the questing shaft of the big buck sodomizing him, and now he was beginning to feel tingles of life in his dangling dingle as the black shaft tickled his insides. He grinned at the Eurasian girl with the shaved groin as he thought how much more obscene this would seem if he committed cunnilingus and passive sodomy at the same time. But before he could order her into position, a telephone rang in the corner.

The Haitian stopped what he was doing. Sir Basil snapped, "Keep buggering me; I'm starting to like it. Ching Lang, hand me the phone." The tawny Eurasian girl did so. She knew her master enjoyed holding innocent conversations as he indulged in crimes against nature. Sir Basil remained on his hands and knees, taking the thrusts of his black lover to the hilt as he picked up the receiver and said, "Numero uno here. Who's calling?"

A feminine voice replied, "This is Indira, reporting in as ordered, Sir Basil."

"Indira? Ah, yes, you're the one I planted aboard the yacht of Greystoke of British Intelligence. Why haven't you called sooner?"

"I haven't had the opportunity, sir. As you know, I've been expecting to serve myself as well as cocktails. This was my first chance to sneak ashore to a safe pay phone. Mr. Greystoke is entertaining a British Intelligence team right at this moment, so I must get back to the party right away."

Sir Basil frowned, hissed, "Faster, Pierre," then told his informant on the phone, "You were stupid to risk slipping away if that was all you had to report. Indira! It's no fresh news to me that Greystoke entertains British Intelligence teams. After all, he's the head of British Intelligence in these parts. I planted you as a sleeper spy. You're just supposed to sleep with the sod until you learn something useful to me!"

"I think I have, Sir Basil. You know that American soldier of fortune, Richard Walker?"

"Captain Gringo? Of course I know him. He doesn't like to work for me. He says he doesn't approve of my goals in life, for some reason. I'm not surprised he's drinking with Greystoke again. They've worked for and against each other on other occasions."

Pierre was entering him at a new angle and it was doing something interesting to his jaded glands. So he said, "It was good of you to call, dear. Now, if that's all you have to say . . ."

"It isn't Sir Basil!" the Anglo-Indian girl at the other end of the line cut in, adding, "I know what the mission is, this time."

Hakim arched his back to take his perversion deeper as he purred, "Ah, why didn't you say so in the beginning? What's my old friend and sometimes foe, Greystoke, up to now?"

Indira giggled and said, "I'd say they were going *down* to something, this time. The team that just came in from London includes some deep-sea divers as well as some electricians and code specialists."

"They mean to do some sort of salvage operation for Her Majesty?"

"No, Sir Basil. They intend to tap the underwater cable running from Cuba to the Mexican mainland! I heard them discussing it as I was serving drinks in the main salon earlier this evening. The plan is to connect a telephone line to the undersea cable off the Yucatán Peninsula and monitor messages between Spanish-occupied Cuba and the Mexican mainland. I thought you'd want to know."

Sir Basil's own shaft was starting to rise, thanks to the unusual but effective prostate massage, but the Merchant of Death hadn't gotten this high in the world by putting pleasure before business. So he said, "You thought right, my dear. Woodbine Arms is selling arms and ammunition to both sides on that distressing island, and everyone knows the Cuba Libre movement has been heating up of late. I see what Whitehall wants to know. I want to know, myself. You did well to call me, Indira."

Then he gave an involuntary moan of pleasure as his jaded genitals started to come fully alive, and, knowing that the distant girl's throaty but sexually calm voice had something to do with it, he purred, "I say, I just had a jolly thought. I want you to come over here right away and join the fun. I don't remember, Indira, have I ever fucked you?"

He could picture her blush as she stammered, "You did when you hired me a year ago, Sir Basil. But if I don't get back to the yacht before they miss me . . ."

"Bosh and twaddle. You'll have more fun over here! Hurry, Indira. I want you here as inspiration. I may even have a friend for you. I like to keep these parties spontaneous, what?"

"Sir Basil, if they find out I'm working for you, they'll kill me!"

"I know. That ought to add spice to your evening, eh? I want you here at once, Indira. That's a direct order, and *I* kill people too!"

He heard her sob, but he hung up before she could protest. He knew she was on her way, and of course he knew better than to send her back so that the other side could question her. But he decided he wouldn't tell her that until later. It would be interesting to watch her try to service Pierre as quickly as possible in order to get back to Greystoke in time. If she moved with true inspiration, he might enjoy her himself for dessert.

He said, "That's enough, Pierre. You can take it out now."

"But, boss," the black pleaded, "I haven't come yet!"

Sir Basil chuckled and replied, "Who said anyone but me was supposed to get any pleasure out of these gatherings? Get out of my arse, you fool. I have some telephone calls to make!"

Aboard the yacht moored against the Belize quay, Captain Gringo was having an after-dinner cigar with his brandy, and enjoying neither. The cigar was a Havana Perfecto and the brandy was Napoleon. But the mission outlined by Greystoke of British Intelligence was being run on the cheap, even for dotty old Queen Vickie. Across the table in the main salon, his sidekick and fellow draftee, Legion-deserter Gaston Verrier, was trying to send Captain Gringo a silent message with his sardonic eyes. Captain Gringo didn't need to be told what Gaston was thinking. Old Gaston was a professional, too, and nobody but this crew of limey greenhorns whom Greystoke wanted them to guard could think the plan made much sense.

Greystoke, the spy master, naturally sat at the head of the table. The rest of the team seated at the table consisted of a half-dozen men who should have known better, and two attractive English girls who seemed to have no sense at all. As Captain Gringo puffed silently, waiting for the other shoe to drop, Greystoke said, "Well, ladies and gentlemen, you all know the basic plan. Do any of you have any suggestions?"

Gaston nodded and said, *"Oui,* I vote we drop the whole *très* tedious thing!"

Greystoke was used to Gaston. So he looked at Captain Gringo and raised an eyebrow. Captain Gringo took the Perfecto out of his mouth and said, "He's right, you know. The hurricane season's coming on. Even if we didn't have to worry about that, you're sending a skeleton crew into the territorial waters of a ruthless dictatorship. *El Presidente* Diaz, the redeemer of Mexico, patrols those waters, Greystoke! He's not as popular with his own people as he is with London and Washington, for reasons that escape me. So he has to worry about gunrunners a lot. That idea about us ghosting along off the Mexican coast in a tub disguised as a native coastal schooner is for the birds! Any Mexican gunboat that spots us will surely suspect us of running aid and comfort to Mexican rebels."

Greystoke looked pained and said, "I assure you, Her Majesty's government has no designs against the stable government of Mexico."

Captain Gringo shrugged and replied, "You know that, I know that. Try telling it to *los federales,* at sea or ashore! If Whitehall's so cozy with Mexico these days, why can't London tell Mexico City it wants to listen in on Cuba's telephone communications? Why all this pussyfooting around? The Diaz government will cooperate with London or Washington. Old Diaz likes to stay in good with the great powers. He's having enough trouble keeping a lid on his own people."

Greystoke sighed and said, "The current Mexican government likes to stay in good with Madrid, too. Even if officials we contacted in Mexico City cooperated sincerely, which is a contradiction in terms when you think about it, Royal Governor Weyler of Cuba has Spanish agents planted all through the Mexican government."

One of the girls across the table, the blond one, smiled brightly as she said, "It's not as if we'll be doing anything to hurt anyone on any side, Captain Walker. Great Britain has no intention of taking sides if there's a real revolution in Cuba this year. Whitehall simply has the need to know what's going on."

Captain Gringo frowned at her and said. "I have the same needs, ma'am. So what are you and this other lady doing on this mission?"

The blonde dimpled and said, "I take shorthand. Miss Manson, here, is an expert at breaking codes."

Captain Gringo had been introduced to the girls on coming aboard. So, although he hadn't paid much attention at the time, if the dark, smart-looking one was Flora Manson, the bubbly blonde was Phoebe Chester. Her chest was okay, but the whole idea was still pretty stupid.

He didn't think anyone else would know, so he turned back to Greystoke and asked, "Why does London have to know, if it's not going to do anything about Butcher Weyler and his new concentration camps either way? More important, I'm still an American. I know the U.S. government is mad at me, but before we go any further, how come you haven't leveled with old President Cleveland about this innocent need to know? There's another undersea cable running from Florida to Cuba, you know."

Greystoke shrugged and said, "We have it tapped already. Our Key West office is working with certain Americans who also have a need to know."

"Swell. So you're not asking me to spy on my own country after all. But in that case, what's the point of this other tap down here?"

"Simple. Conversations between Cuba and the U.S. tend to be in English and don't tell us anything we don't already know or assume. Your officials in Washington are

13

divided about what's to be done about the Cuban situation, but they're leaning, if at all, to the Cuban Republican party of Palma and Marti. Tomas Estrada Palma is practically running the Cuba Libre movement from New York, with the poet, Marti, writing blow-by-blow descriptions of the various guerrilla activities and Spanish reprisals to be published by the Hearst newspaper syndicate."

"So why doesn't Queen Victoria just subscribe to the *Examiner?* What are we supposed to find out, tapping public communications lines?"

Greystoke shrugged and said, "We don't know. That's why we want to listen in. Washington and London were both caught by surprise when Spain suddenly replaced the reasonably civilized Royal Governor Campos with Butcher Weyler and his cutthroat crew. We still don't grasp just what those so-called concentration camps Weyler's invented really are, although, to hear the rebels, they sound rather grim."

Gaston said, *"Merde alors,* I can tell you what will happen in the end. The Cuban rebels are getting help from American sympathizers. In a year or so the rebels will have the arms and supplies to mount a full-scale revolt. The Spaniards will send in even greater forces, and the Americans will get excited and back the Cuba Libre movement openly."

"That would mean war!" said another man at the table.

Gaston nodded and said, "But of course. The U.S. has been looking for an excuse to have a war with Spain for years."

Greystoke stared at the tip of his own cigar as he mused, "A Spanish-American War? Sounds rather mad, even for the Yanks. But, as we sit here talking about it, whatever will happen really should be getting through to Whitehall. The Foreign Office doesn't really like to guess blindly about such matters. So let's forget the reason for your mission and get on with the ways and means, eh what?"

He stabbed his cigar at Captain Gringo and said, "You all know Captain Walker and his associate, M'sieur Verrier. They and the Maxim machine guns we've issued will provide security should you bump into unwashed pirate types up the coast."

Gaston asked, "What if we run into Dick's Mexican gunboat?"

But the dapper spy master ignored him to say, "Lieutenant Carmichael, as our master diver, you'd know better than I if the diving gear we've issued to you will suffice, eh what?"

Carmichael, a burly Scot with a hint of Glasgow in his almost Cambridge accent, nodded and said, "The waters are shallow where we're going, if the charts mean anything. The diving suits are new and tested to two hundred feet. Those coral flats the cable runs across for miles off the Mexican coast are under less than eighty feet of water."

"Water full of sharks," Gaston chimed in sarcastically.

Carmichael wrinkled his red drinker's nose and said, "So I've been told. But since you won't be diving, let *me* worry about the local flora and fauna. I've dived in the Med, off Gib, and I must say the few sharks I ever met seemed a cowardly lot."

"*Eh bien,* have you ever been introduced to Caribbean sharks, or, for that matter, our quaint barracudas?"

Captain Gringo said, "Knock it off, Gaston. The man just said he hasn't got a hard hat for you, and I'm still more worried about *federales* than fish. Listen, Greystoke, is there any chance we could take along something more serious than small arms?"

Greystoke looked pained and answered, "The converted schooner's timbers wouldn't take the pounding of a deck gun. But not to worry, Dick. I've seen the awesome results of your machine-gun skills!"

"Bullshit. Sorry, ladies. It's easy for you to say not to worry. You get to stay here while you send us out to play hide-and-seek with the Mexican navy! I want at least a few cases of dynamite. Can do?"

"I suppose so, old boy, but whatever for? What do you mean to do with dynamite if I get you some?"

"Don't know. But if I think of something, I'll probably want it in a hurry."

Gaston chuckled fondly and recalled, "I saw him sink a Brazilian gunboat with dynamite one time. Not on the high seas, of course. But he is a *très* ingenious lad."

Greystoke nodded and started to say something else as he looked around with his empty glass in his hand. A Tonkinese serving wench materialized to refill it for him. Greystoke nodded his thanks, then frowned and asked her, "I say, what are you doing here, Joy Yin? Where's Indira?"

The Oriental girl looked confused and replied, "I am not knowing, sir. Steward is sending me out to serving you when he no can find Indira."

Greystoke shrugged and turned back to rejoin the conversation. But Captain Gringo had been listening. He asked, "Are we talking about that nice-looking Hindu gal I noticed the last time I was aboard, Greystoke?"

Greystoke nodded and said, "Yes. She must be brooding in her cabin or some such rot. She's a rather moody little wog. Why do you ask?"

"You'd better make sure she's still aboard."

Greystoke looked blank and said, "Aboard? Of course she's aboard." And then, because he was, after all, paid to think fast, Greystoke turned to the little Tonk and said, "Tell the steward I want to see Indira, chop chop!"

Joy Yin left in a hurry. She looked even nicer from the

rear. The brunette English girl, Flora Manson, seemed to think fast, too. She asked Captain Gringo with a puzzled little frown, "Have I missed something? Who cares if some serving girl or other is off in a corner somewhere?"

Captain Gringo said, "It depends on who she's serving, and where she's gone. Being an uncouth Yank gives me certain advantages over you spies who've grown up with lots of hired help. I've never gotten used to talking about everything from my sex life to an espionage mission in front of semi-invisible servants. That Hindu gal was serving dinner while Greystoke was outlining the plans of this mission, remember?"

Greystoke gasped and asked, "Are you suggesting someone's paid little Indira to listen in on my dinner conversations, Dick?"

"Why not? Don't you guys have British agents peeling spuds for the young kaiser, or maybe fluffing up his pillows? If you don't, you're sure missing an easy bet!"

Greystoke looked pained. He said, "Rubbish. I've had Indira for some time, and, dash it all, she's a British subject!"

Captain Gringo just grinned. He suspected he knew all too well how long and in what positions Greystoke had had the nicely stacked Anglo-Indian girl. He'd always wondered why salesmen had no sales resistance or why tinhorn gamblers never seemed to suspect anyone else in the game of cheating.

The bubbly blonde, Phoebe said, "Pooh, who ever heard of a wog spy? Who on earth would the perishing girl be working for besides us?"

Captain Gringo shrugged and answered, "How many other countries are there? I can think of a lot of people who'd be more interested in the current Cuban situation than I am. But, hey, let's not worry about it until we find out whether the girl's still on board or not."

She wasn't. The English steward came in, wearing a

white jacket and a worried expression, and told Grey-stoke, 'Indira doesn't seem to be anywhere about, sir. Nobody saw her slip ashore, but . . .'"

"Tell Crosby and Singh to go after her!" Greystoke cut in, as Captain Gringo slid back his chair and rose to his considerable height.

Gaston was already rising as the big blond American said, "Let's go, Gaston."

So the dapper little Frenchman nodded at their host and said, "We thank you for a most enjoyable dinner, M'sieur Greystoke."

They were out on deck and headed for the gangplank when Greystoke caught up with them. The Britisher caught Captain Gringo by the arm and demanded, "Hold on, Walker. Where do you think you're going?"

Captain Gringo said, "I don't know. Costa Rica, I suppose. It's about the only place there's not a price on my head that's easy to get to from here."

"Don't be an ass! What about the mission?"

"What mission, Greystoke? Can't you see it's off? I thought you went to spy school. Didn't anybody ever tell you that you're supposed to scrub an operation the other side knows all about?"

Greystoke snapped, "Don't be ridiculous! My lads will pick her up within minutes. How far can a barefoot lass in a sari get without being spotted in Central America?"

Captain Gringo shrugged and replied, "How far does she have to get? Thanks to Alexander Graham Bell, it's not like the good old days when you and I were young, Maggie. We live in changing times. It's almost the twenti-eth century, and you're right about people chatting back and forth on those undersea cables you're so interested in. Your serving wench had a good half-hour lead on us before you noticed she was missing. By now she could have repeated our dinner conversation to Butcher Weyler, the Mexican Secret Service, or, hell, the Tsar of All the

Russians! Meanwhile, you don't even know who she was working for. So thanks a lot, but no thanks. The mission sounded shoestring and spooky even before we knew for sure that other people we don't know seem interested in it!"

Gaston chimed in, *"Mes oui,* a soldier of fortune accepts certain risks. But suicide is not one of them, *hein?"*

Greystoke shook his head and said, "I'll not let you go. Have you two forgotten you could be arrested here in British Honduras, if I wasn't, ah, your employer?"

Captain Gringo hadn't, but he said, "That would be dumb, even for you, Greystoke. If you turned us in to the British constabulary, they'd ask you lots of questions, too. I thought you professional sneaks liked to keep your business from your fellow Brits."

Greystoke said, "We do. We like to carry out our missions, too! Without you two along as security officers, the cable tap doesn't stand a chance. So London and I will be very annoyed if you back out now. And what the hell —if we can't be useful to Her Majesty, here, we may as well at least offer the local police a helping hand, eh what?"

Captain Gringo shot Gaston a look. The Frenchman shook his head and said *"Mes non.* If we kill him in the middle of town, we'll never get away from his *très fatigue* fellow agents."

Captain Gringo nodded, but said, "That's naked blackmail, Greystoke."

Greystoke smiled thinly and replied, "They taught me *that* at spy school too. The mission is still on, and you two are still going along to guard my people. As one of your Indian chiefs said, I have spoken."

"God damn it, Greystoke, I know you don't give a shit what happens to Gaston and me. But can't you see you're risking those other Englishmen and two English girls as well?"

"My lot knew they'd be called on to take risks when they volunteered for British Intelligence. There's an outside chance Indira just jumped ship, you know."

"Oh, sure, she got homesick, right? Tell me something —where do you catch the streetcar to Calcutta in this banana port? Somebody *planted* that dame on you, Greystoke!"

Greystoke shrugged and said, "It's beginning to look that way. But let's not get the wind up, Yank. For all we know, she was working for some curious friendly power."

"Or Spain, or Mexico, or anybody at all who doesn't want you listening in on their private communications."

"We'll cross that bridge when we come to it, Walker."

Captain Gringo scowled down at the Englishman and asked, "What's this *we* shit? You won't be going up the coast with us, will you?"

"Hardly. I have to stay here and coordinate Her Majesty's over-all operations in this hemisphere. Naturally I mean to follow up on Indira's mysterious dash into the night. Meanwhile, you and the others are to carry on as ordered and let me worry about minor difficulties."

Captain Gringo started to say he didn't consider sailing into a trap a minor difficulty, but he saw that Greystoke was determined, and Greystoke had them by the balls. So he sighed and said, "Okay, let's figure out how the fuck we're going to do it without getting killed."

Greystoke had renamed the disguised yacht *Flamenco Lass*. Greystoke was like that. But her name was not the problem.

Flamenco Lass was an oil-burning auxiliary schooner, built on the bonny banks of Clyde, but obviously not to go roaming in the gloaming. She was a high-strung racing craft and she looked it. Her slim funnel was as sharply raked as her masts, and anyone could see that she had high-pressure boilers in a time and area where any kind of auxiliary power was seldom seen with sail. British Intelligence had stained her expensive new sails with some tea-colored gunk and painted her hull a nondescript shade of cow chip. But she still looked like she was making at least fifteen knots, at anchor.

Nobody who knew these waters was going to make her out a native trading schooner. She looked as Mosquito Coast as a Gibson Girl, and as tempting a prize to any admiring Latin with a gun. Captain Gringo had noticed there were a lot of guys like that in this neighborhood, too.

But he knew it was fruitless to argue about the figure of the pretty gringa with Greystoke. Greystoke was like that, too. So he and Gaston followed the others aboard with their gear, and as the tide went out, so did *Flamenco Lass*.

Nothing happened for a while. Nothing ever happened as long as there were British gunboats in the area, and the port of Belize was the capital of British Honduras. So as their skipper, a Royal Navy type named Boggs, who somehow managed to look like he was standing for inspection even in the battered seaman's cap and striped shirt he wore, conned the *Flamenco Lass* up the coast, Captain Gringo made a tour to familiarize himself with the vessel he'd been told to guard with his life and two Maxims.

The machine guns and their ammo were still stored in the main salon, now converted to a workshop with the diving gear and other spy stuff. Captain Gringo meant to let them stay there until they were out of sight from shore. The damnedest people poked around in the mangroves along the Mosquito Coast for turtle eggs, Spanish moss, or anything else they could sell to the highest bidder.

There was no problem about where to mount the rear gun. There was a nice flat expanse of coaming behind the cockpit. The Maxim could be set up there, and the gun crew would be protected from the shoulders down by the cockpit bulkhead. The helm was a double wheel, running through the big boxy binnacle. The helmsman would be protected from fire astern if he manned the forward wheel, when and if.

Finding a position for the bow gun was another matter. The yacht was built on the lines of a Bluenose schooner. Her bows came to a sharp point behind her bowsprit, which offered problems in traversing the gun and no cover from anyone shooting back. There was an ankle-high timber bulwark along the edges of the triangular foredeck. There was an almost-flush hatch cover and an anchor winch too low slung to be anything but something to trip over. In other words, there wasn't any decent cover forward of the cabin bulkhead. A machine-gun crew up there would be fully exposed. There had to be a better way.

Captain Gringo drifted aft, pausing to light a smoke as he leaned against the hip-high cabin roof. He heard feminine voices. There was nobody within earshot on deck. The sounds were coming from a ventilation funnel, magnified by the hornlike metal tube. He knew he was listening in on the two English girls Greystoke had insisted on sending along. Captain Gringo wasn't usually interested in hen-party talk, so he started to move on. But then he heard the blonde say, "That big Yank is rather nice-looking, in a brutal way. Have you made any plans regarding him, Flora?"

The more intelligent brunette replied, "Good Lord, Phoebe, don't you ever think of anything else? We've barely left port and haven't even unpacked yet."

"Pooh, I know where we are. It's where we're going that I'm interested in. If you don't want the big Yank, I do."

Captain Gringo heard an annoyed sniff, followed by, "You're welcome to him, I'm sure. But what about you and that handsome merchant captain you seemed so fond of in Belize?"

"Pooh, I'm still fond of him. But, as you just said, he's in Belize. How do you think we'd better work it, Flora? I mean, it might be awkward, about the bunks and all."

Flora Manson made a noise that was something between a laugh and a sneer before she said, "You're on your own, Phoebe. I'll be damned if I can see how you'll need my help in romancing that big brute. And I'll be damned if I'm about to let you bed him in here, too!"

"Oh, dear, I was afraid you'd be a spoilsport. Honestly, Flora, where can a girl, well, meet a friend in private aboard this dinky little boat?"

"I'm sure you'll work something out, dear. Just don't tell me about it when you do it. It's not that I'm a prude. I just don't believe in mixing business with pleasure, and this is a serious business we're on for Her Majesty, what?"

"Pooh, you repeat the messages and I'll take them down. You know I'm a wizard at shorthand. But, heavens, we may be out on this mission for weeks, and a girl has feelings, you know."

Captain Gringo shook his head wearily and started to move on. He felt a little guilty about eavesdropping, and wasn't hearing anything that surprised him much in any case. But then the bubbly blonde asked her quieter, darker, and obviously smarter companion, "'Fess up, Flora. How *do* you cope with the problem? You're not a virgin, are you?"

Flora laughed ruefully and answered, "Hardly. You know I took this job after my husband was killed on a similar mission. I have, ah, feelings, too. But, as I said, I try to put them aside when I'm on the job."

Captain Gringo nodded in approval. Old Flora sounded like a smart little dame. She was prettier than dumb Phoebe, too, damn it.

He'd heard enough. He moved on aft, smiling crookedly as he saw the humor in the situation. Wasn't that life, for you? The dames you could have for the asking never seemed to be the ones you wanted. He wondered how he was going to deal with Phoebe when she made her inevitable pass.

He shrugged and decided he'd deal with temptation the sensible way. By giving in to it. As the days wore on, it would help to steady his own nerves to know that if he really needed some, it was there. Meanwhile, like Flora Manson, he thought it better to keep his mind on the mission. Sooner or later, you always got laid. But once you were killed, it was for keeps.

He joined Gaston, the helmsman, and Captain Boggs in the cockpit. Gaston was bitching about something. Gaston was always bitching about something, but as Captain Gringo picked up the threads of the conversation, he saw that Gaston was making sense.

The dispute was over the heading. Boggs was coasting within rifle shot of the soggy, mangrove-haunted mainland shore to their left. Gaston thought this was a lousy idea. Captain Gringo agreed. He said, "You're the master, Boggs. But if I were you, I'd be standing farther out to sea."

Boggs replied, in a clipped and proper manner, "You're not me, Captain Walker. My charts show a bewildering confusion of shoals and coral keys running in line with the mainline coast. Some of the perishing reefs and islands seem to be vaguely charted, too! I say, what is one to make of a series of perishing ink dots marked 'suspected shoal'?"

"Worry about them a lot," said Captain Gringo. Then he added, "Look, I know the waters to the north are badly charted. The damned coral sand shifts around a few miles with every hurricane. On the other hand, there are unmarked shoals along the mainland coast, too, and those mangrove keys have a mind of their own. Meanwhile, we're cruising in plain view of anyone on shore."

"What of it? It's my understanding the Mosquito Coast is mostly uninhabited jungle."

"It is, but 'mostly' isn't good enough, Boggs. Aside from chicle gatherers and such, there are telegraph and telephone lines running up and down the coast these days. Anybody working for the other side can send a message from the nearest village. Meanwhile, almost nobody lives on the smaller offshore keys, and those who do don't have telephones, see?"

Boggs shrugged, snapped, "Two points to windward!" to his enlisted helmsman, then asked Captain Gringo, sarcastically, "Are you satisfied now?"

Captain Gringo shook his head and said, "No. I notice we're sending up a plume of funnel smoke. It's not a heavy plume. But may I ask why we're showing off our engines at all?"

Boggs frowned and replied. "We're showing funnel smoke because our auxiliary power is adding a few knots to our speed, of course. Isn't that what auxiliary power is supposed to do?"

"Not when it doesn't have to. Aside from telling the whole world we have steam power before we may want to use it as an ace in the hole, you're wasting fuel we may need later. Meanwhile, the trades are blowing hard and steady from abeam, and a fore-'n'-aft rig like ours is meant to sail fast and forever with the wind abeam."

Boggs didn't bother to repress a sneer as he answered, "We've plenty of bunker fuel, and my orders are to get you lot there as quickly as possible."

Captain Gringo shrugged and said, "You're the boss. I'm sure the Mexican navy will sell us oil if we need it to get away from them in a hurry. I'd like to borrow a couple of your crewmen to help me shift some boxes. Is that okay with you?"

"It depends. Just what did you have in mind, Walker?"

"Barricade. Up in the bows. Want to have some boxes of canned goods between the machine gun position and anybody trying to sweep it off that exposed foredeck."

Boggs frowned and asked, "Won't that make an awful mess? I mean, the very idea of a bullet hitting a tin of tomatoes sounds rather ghastly!"

"Yeah. Meanwhile, said tomatoes can take a bullet with a lot less pain than living flesh. We used that dodge a lot, fighting Apache. You may lose a few pounds of food. But you live longer, even hungry. Remember, we don't stand to lose even an ounce of grub unless somebody's trying very hard to kill us."

Boggs shook his head and said, "The first green water over the bows would wash all the supplies overboard long before they could serve as a bullet shield."

"Not if we nail the boxes to the decking."

Boggs looked thunderstruck and gasped, *"Nail,* you say? Nail packing crates to a teakwood deck? Unthinkable! I promised to get this yacht back safe and sound and shipshape, Walker! Can't have perishing nail holes in that expensive decking, what?"

Gaston said, *"Merde alors,* let's jump overboard and get it over with, Dick. These people most obviously have *trés fatigue* horns of the green."

Lieutenant Carmichael came up from below to make a liar of Gaston. Carmichael said he was satisfied with the way his diving gear was stored and asked if there were any other smart moves to make. That got him into the argument about a forward barricade. Carmichael said it sounded like a splendid idea and seemed as disgusted as the two soldiers of fortune when Boggs protested marring the woodwork.

Carmichael said, "You can't be serious, Captain Boggs! Should the other side spot us up the coast, they'll surely drive worse things than nails into this vessel!"

Boggs sniffed and said, "We'll cross that bridge when we come to it. I'm not an unreasonable chap. I'm perfectly willing to accept minor damage to my ship if there's no way around it. But I see no need to muck it up with deck cargo and bash the bright work full of perishing spikes before we've seen any sign of danger."

He turned to Captain Gringo and added, "You may as well install your guns in position, provided you do no damage to *Flamenco Lass*."

Captain Gringo shook his head and said, "Not unless you have someone else in mind to man either gun. Waving guns about in plain sight of a lee shore has a funny effect on other guys with guns of their own. I want both Maxims firing from cover, if they fire at all. If we can't have cover, what the fuck's the point?"

"He's right," said Carmichael, adding, "While we're on the subject, Walker, how do you mean to man both guns at once? I mean, if one's in the bow and one's in the stern . . ."

"I commute," said Captain Gringo. "Hopefully, anyone after us will attack from astern, abeam, or ahead. In a pinch, Gaston, here, can handle one gun pretty good while I do the honors with whichever one seems to be in the best position."

"I thought it took two men to man a machine gun."

"One guy feeding and changing belts as the other fires is the best way, but not the only way, Carmichael. We're more likely to have a running fight than a standoff from fixed positions. Bobbing around out here, we'll most likely only manage occasional short bursts. A solo gunner can handle the likely targets."

Carmichael frowned and asked, "Oh? What sort of targets are you used to along the Mosquito Coast, chaps?"

Captain Gringo shrugged and said, "Unreconstructed Indians in seagoing canoes. Maybe leftover coastal pirates in another sailboat. They tend to get discouraged after they take one good burst of machine-gun fire."

Boggs asked, "What about gunboats, Walker?" Captain Gringo laughed and said, "Shit, we're not about to stand off a gunboat or even a serious revenue cutter with two lousy Maxims and a wooden hull!"

"In that case, what are we to do if we run into one?"

"Surrender, or run like hell for shoal water and hope they miss with their first few shells. This schooner's not a man-o'-war, Boggs. So, about that oil-smoke plume you're shitting up the horizon line with . . ."

Boggs swore under his breath and moved the brass telegraph handle near the wheel to signal the engine room. But then Gaston sighed and said, "Perhaps we are being hasty, my children. Regard the horizon to our south!"

All but the helmsman turned to follow Gaston's gaze aft. Captain Gringo muttered, "Oh, shit," as he made out the dark lateen sails of a long black vessel, gaining on them fast.

Gaston was already making for the hatchway forward of the cockpit. So Captain Gringo called after him, "Be sure and bring at least three belts of ammo, too!"

As Gaston dropped out of sight, Boggs said, "I say, I don't like the look of that xebec, either. But aren't we acting a bit dramatic at this stage of the game? I don't see any overt signs of hostility yet."

Captain Gringo said, "Waiting for hostile signs can take fifty years off a guy's life. That's not a xebec. It's a Carib sailing canoe. That doesn't mean it's manned by Indians, of course. Lots of guys in a hurry scoot up and down the Mosquito Coast in a lateen-rigged Carib. But friendly merchant vessels are supposed to show their colors as they sail, and I don't see a flag back there. Do you?"

Boggs shrugged and answered, "Twaddle. Half these perishing Hispanic types don't have proper papers. The bum boats back in Belize were poled or sailed about the harbor by bloody women and children."

"Yeah, but that's not a bum boat gaining on us, Boggs. It's a seagoing vessel, sailing close-hauled by a skipper who seems to know his craft. And, like I said, you're supposed to fly your colors in these waters."

Boggs glanced aloft at the British merchant flag flapping in the trades. Then Carmichael said, "I say, they *are* running up a flag."

The mystery vessel was. It was the same red signal as *Flamenco Lass* was sporting. Boggs said, "Rubbish. That can't be a *British* vessel!"

Gaston came back with the Maxim cradled across his chest, tripod and looped ammo belts hanging down. Captain Gringo moved to help him with it, and, without exchanging more than a few grunts, the two soldiers of fortune manhandled the heavy weapon into place in the windward corner of the cockpit.

By this time some of the others, including the two English girls, had started to come out on deck. Captain Gringo yelled, "Everyone below, and for chrissake stay there! I do mean everybody. Gaston, get on the safe side of the binnacle and man the helm. Boggs, you and these other two guys better get below or hit the deck."

Carmichael produced a pistol from under his linen jacket and dropped to one knee. The enlisted helmsman looked at Boggs. Boggs said, "Steady as she goes. I'm in command of this vessel, Walker."

Captain Gringo said, "You're an asshole, too. Gaston, you know the form." Then the tall American dropped to

29

his knees behind the machine gun and began to load and prime it. Gaston sat down with his back to the cockpit coaming, watching the helmsman as he lit a smoke.

The sinister, low-slung vessel was moving faster than a sailing craft was supposed to, taking water over her low needle bow as her skipper drove her recklessly close-hauled through the light chop, which they hardly felt on the bigger, more sensibly sailed schooner. Boggs murmured, "I say, that's a wonky way to sail. They must be half awash at the rate their taking it green over the bows."

"They have plenty of guys to bail," said Captain Gringo, adding, "Those aren't coconuts peeking over the free-board at us. Have you ever seen a native bum boat or fisherman with a crew that size?"

"Hmm, they do seem to have a reason for being so low in the water. Whoever they may be, they have no right to fly the British merchant ensign. If that skipper has a master's rating issued by our merchant marine, he's certainly forgotten a lot of his rules and regs. Why, dash it all, that xebec doesn't even have proper Plimsoll marks to show his proper waterline! Do you think he's flying false colors?"

Captain Gringo smiled thinly and replied, "What can I tell you? They gave up flying the skull and crossbones years ago."

The other vessel was within hailing distance now. So Captain Gringo yelled in Spanish, "That's close enough!" and a hoarse voice called back, "Aw, is that any way to talk, señor? We wish for to inspect your papers. We are British customs, understand?"

Captain Gringo didn't bother to yell back that he understood, indeed. He trained his sights on the center of the triangular foresail and fired a short burst through the dark canvas to, A, let them know they'd picked the wrong prey, and, B, keep the noise down in case anyone was within earshot on the not-too-distant shore.

They must have been unusually stupid or unusually anxious. They kept coming. A rifle squibbed in the bow of the low-slung whatever, and something hummed like an angry hornet past Captain Gringo's right shoulder. So he growled a curse, lowered the muzzle of his Maxim, and raked the hull with a long, savage burst of automatic fire.

The Carib craft broached suddenly broadside to his fire as someone let go of the helm, and the wind-filled lateen sails weather-vaned in the trades. Anyone he hadn't hit had ducked below the low sides, of course, so he gave them a traverse of hot lead along the waterline from stem to stern, then swept the other way for luck, and as white water spouted along the black hull, a white cloth started waving above the bulwarks back there.

Captain Gringo ceased fire as the space between the two vessels began to open rapidly. He looked over his shoulder to ask, "Everybody okay?"

That's when he saw that Gaston was manning the helm. Boggs had taken cover next to Carmichael. The poor slob whom Boggs had ordered to remain at the helm was down, too. But he wasn't taking cover. He didn't need it. He lay face down with a big blob of raspberry jam where one of his shoulder blades used to be. Captain Gringo raised an eyebrow at Gaston. The Frenchman said, *"Oui. As anyone but a species of fool should have known, one always aims at the helmsman with the first round, non?"*

Boggs looked like a man who was having a bad dream and wondering why he couldn't wake up as he muttered, "They killed him! The bastards killed him! They'll hang for this!"

Captain Gringo looked aft before he muttered, "No, they won't. Damn, I was going to suggest going back to question any survivors, but you were right. They must have already had a lot of water inboard."

As the others followed his gaze, they saw that the trades had flattened the lateen sails against the water and the hull was already below the surface. A couple of dots were still bobbing around back there. But as Carmichael said, "We could still pick up one of those swimmers," one head went under. Carmichael spotted a shark fin moving toward another and gasped, "Oh, I say!"

Gaston said dryly, *"Oui,* blood in the water has that effect on our cowardly local sharks. Who do you think they were, Dick?"

Captain Gringo began to clean the action of his Maxim as he shrugged and answered, "We'll never know for sure, now. I hope they were just pirates. It's a little early for anybody else to be trying to intercept us."

Carmichael said, "They didn't follow us out of Belize. I told you I used to work in the Med between Malta and Gib. I'd have noticed a lateen rig if there'd been any in the harbor."

"Yeah, they came out of a mangrove cove. They were waiting for us. I hope it wasn't us in particular. But you never know. This goddamn schooner's easy enough to describe, despite her half-ass disguise."

Gaston said, *"Oui.* We must do something to change her outline. Perhaps if the masts had less rake?"

Bogg shook his head like a bull with a fly between his horns and snapped, "Don't be ridiculous. In the first place, we couldn't without shipyard facilities. In the second, it would throw her out of trim!"

"Merde alors, do we want to go fast or do we want to get there without a series of *très fatigue* running sea fights?"

Captain Gringo said, "Knock it off, guys. You're both right. It would take days in a shipyard to really disguise this tub. There has to be a better way."

The vessel he'd smoked up had sunk completely now. He glanced down at the dead helmsman and added, "We'd better think about wrapping this poor guy in his oilskins and sliding him over the side, too."

Boggs snapped, "We'll do no such thing! I'm getting tired of having to remind you who's in command of this vessel, Walker!"

Captain Gringo shrugged and said, "Command it, then. I don't care if you give him a regular sea burial or shove him up your ass. But you're going to have to do something. It's too hot and humid to just let him lie there!"

The others aboard had been kept below by the gunfire, of course. But now that it had stopped, they started popping back on deck. Boggs ordered another man to relieve Gaston at the helm and told two others to get a tarp and wrap their dead crewmate in it.

So far, so good. Then the blonde, Phoebe Chester, spotted the corpse from where she stood in the hatchway and let out a banshee scream. Captain Gringo muttered, "See what I mean?"

Flora Manson wasn't as noisy, but she didn't really show much more sense as she pushed past Phoebe and ran over to the fallen helmsman. Captain Gringo called out, "Don't kneel!" But Flora did anyway, and put the knee of her skirt smack in the thick crimson goo oozing out from under the dead man as she tried to help him. She looked up, stricken, to sob, "Oh, my God, I think he's dead!"

Gaston was closer to her, so he helped her to her feet as the others roled the limp corpse onto the tarp. Gaston said, "M'mselle really must learn to pay attention, *hein?* When one is told not to do something, it is usually for a good reason. But cold water will take that blood out of your linen if you see to it before it dries."

Flora looked down, saw the stain on her white skirt, and gagged. As she pulled away and dashed below, Phoebe stamped her foot at Gaston and said, "You upset her, you brute!"

Gaston protested, "Me? I did nothing to anyone, m'selle!" But then Phoebe dashed below, too. So Gaston shrugged at Captain Gringo and said, "I was only trying to be *pratique*. Did I say something wrong?"

Captain Gringo shook his head and said, "Don't worry about it." Then he turned to Boggs and said, "For a guy with such a short fuse, you seem to be doing just what I suggested."

Boggs snapped, "I'll be damned if I am. You suggested dropping him over the side to those sharks. We'll put in at the next port of call to give him a proper Christian burial!"

"Are you *loco en la cabeza*, Boggs? The next port of call is Corozal!"

"I'm well aware of that, Walker. Corozal is still British Honduras. We can see that our lad is given proper Anglican rites and a burial in hallowed Protestant ground."

Captain Gringo shook his head wearily and growled, "Forgive my asking. I can see you *are loco en la cabeza!* I can see you haven't been in the spy trade long."

"I don't consider myself a spy. I'm sailing master of this vessel."

"Yeah, there I go asking dumb questions again. Okay, I'll use small words and you can stop me if I'm going too fast for you, Boggs. This mission wasn't my idea. We're working for British Intelligence. You got that? British Intelligence, not British *Stupidity*. The reason Greystoke put this mission together in Belize instead of Corozal wasn't to make us sail a few miles farther. The mission was supposed to be a secret, see?"

"I'm well aware of the reason for the rest of you lot going on this perishing mission, damm it!"

"You weren't planning on coming along? Look, Boggs, Corozal is a border town. You savvy what is a border town? Mexican customs men, spies, God knows who, watching the border. If we put into Corozal, people are

34

going to notice us. Bad people. Guys on the other side. Am I talking too fast for you?"

Boggs snapped, "Don't patronize me, you Yankee ruffian! I bloody well know what my duties are to this vessel, passengers, and crew. One of my crew has just died for England, and, by God, England is going to bury him right!"

Captain Gringo muttered, "Hang some crêpe on your nose. Your brain just died."

Then Gaston took him by the elbow and steered him back toward the machine gun as the others finished lashing the corpse in the tarp. The older Frenchman murmured, "Give it up, Dick. We had an officer like that at the siege of Camerone."

"The asshole's trying to get us all killed!"

"That is what I just said. There is no use arguing with the species. Men like Boggs are immune to *logique.*"

"I noticed. So what do you suggest? What did you do about the officer who tried to get you Legion guys killed in Mexico that time?"

"We paid no attention to him, of course. After a time the Juristas were kind enough to shoot the idiot, and those of us still alive were able to surrender in peace. The Mexicans were much more reasonable about things at the siege of Camerone."

Captain Gringo fished out a smoke and lit it before he said, "You were dealing with Mexicans under Juarez. The guys working for Diaz make me nervous. I didn't sign up for this voyage to surrender to anybody. But if that asshole keeps on this way . . ."

"*Oui,* he will, as you say, get us all killed. But look at the bright side, Dick. The man just said he wanted to put in at Corozal."

Captain Gringo blew smoke out both nostrils as he stared down at the smaller man to ask, "Are you nuts, too?

Corozal's the spy crosssroads of this coast! Once we sail in their with a stiff on board to explain to British customs anybody who hasn't got us spotted by now . . ."

"Ferme la bouche!" Gaston cut in, adding, *"Sacre* God damn, I am trying to talk sense, and you keep cursing a species of insect we agree on! This mission, as I said in the beginning, is doomed as well as foolish! We were forced to come along, but only because that *très fatigue* Greystoke had us by the hairs where they are short."

Captain Gringo suddenly grinned and said, "Gotcha. Greystoke and the muscle he has to twist our arms with are back in Belize. Is it our fault his own skipper wants to put us ashore in Corozal?"

"Mes non! I heard you beg him, just now, not to put in there at all!"

Captain Gringo took a drag on his cigar as he stared aft, thinking of loose ends. There were a lot of them. Greystoke was going to be mad as hell. Greystoke had agents all over Latin America. On the other hand, a running head start before Greystoke could guess they were gone would beat any chance this half-ass mission had. He nodded and said, "Okay. We hang innocent and see what's going on in Corozal these days before we make a break for it."

Captain Gringo had the stern Maxim cleaned and covered with a tarp when a big wet toad plopped down on his head, turned into a big wet eel, and slithered down his spine. Another golf-ball-sized raindrop sizzled his cigar out. So he muttered, "Shit," and headed below. Boggs and his new helmsman were welcome to stay on deck as they steered for Corozal. He felt sorry for the enlisted man, but he hoped Boggs would drown in the coming rain squall.

By the time he reached the small stateroom he shared with Gaston, the rain was tap dancing merrily on the low overhead. Gaston wasn't there. Captain Gringo couldn't blame him. Despite or perhaps because of the tropic rain, the stateroom was as warm and muggy as a bathroom after someone had taken a hot shower. He couldn't open the port because the stateroom was on the lee side and Boggs was sailing close-hauled with the lee rail almost under. It was damp enough in here without risking gouts of green water through an open port.

He wasn't particularly tired. On the other hand, there was nothing better to do, and a knock-around guy never knew when he was going to have to stay up all night. So he hung his gun rig over the bunk, peeled off his damp duds, and flopped atop the covers to mayhaps catch some shut-eye.

He closed his eyes, but nothing happened. He had too much on his mind for a daylight nap. He lit another smoke but remained supine on the bunk, as he ran plan after plan through his bemused mind. None of them worked.

Captain Gringo didn't like the idea of desertion. He had his professional reputation to consider. On the other hand, he didn't fancy the idea of getting killed, and, with Boggs in command, this mission was an exercise in textbook wrong moves. Greystoke couldn't have picked a worse sailing master if he'd asked the Spanish government for one.

That was an interesting thought. But Boggs was hard to buy as a Spanish spy. Anything was possible. But it seemed more likely the guy was simply a rule-book skipper who lacked the imagination it took to do things sneakily. It hardly mattered, either way. Whether Boggs was working for British or Spanish Intelligence, the results would be the same. Once they showed their hand in Corozal, any other players in the Great Game would be able to cover all bets.

There was a discreet tap on the door. He'd left it unlocked for Gaston. But that wasn't Gaston's knock. So he covered his lap with a pillow and called out, *"Entrada."*

The door opened, and the blonde, Phoebe Chester, slipped in to quickly close and lock it behind her. She was wearing nothing but a blue silk kimono. Somehow that didn't surprise Captain Gringo. He sat up, keeping the pillow in place, as she gasped, "Oh, you're not dressed!"

He patted the sheets beside him and answered, "Neither are you. Sit down and take a load off your mind. What can I do for you, doll face?"

He thought it was a dumb question, but he'd been raised polite.

The bubbly blonde came over and sat beside him, of course, but she seemed to feel that she had to say, "I can only stay a minute. I wouldn't have come at all if I'd known you were in bed."

He put his free arm around her waist as he nodded and said, "Right. You have something important you want to talk about, eh?"

She didn't pull away, but her face turned a becoming shade of pink as she said, "You sure are fresh. But I know you're just joshing. I wanted to talk to you in private because I'm worried about that silly Captain Boggs."

"Why? Has he been getting fresh with you, too?"

"Be serious. I couldn't help overhearing some of the argument you were having with him about putting in at Corozal. I can't for the life of me see why he means to take such a chance. Even I can see that's not the way one keeps a secret mission a secret."

"Yeah, I told him even a bubble brain could see that. But what do you expect me to do about it, honey? I'm only in charge of security, not navigation. It's up to old Boggs to say where we go or don't go in this tub."

The blonde snuggled into a more comfortable position against him as she said, "Pooh, everyone else aboard agrees he's being silly. I'm sure that if you seized command from him, none of the others would object."

Captain Gringo shook his head, snuffed out his cigar, and said, "They call that mutiny on the high seas, doll face. It's sort of frowned upon."

"Even if the rest of the crew votes to elect a new master?"

"You've been talking to people, haven't you? It's still no dice, doll. A ship at sea is not a democracy. It's under international sea law, which is an absolute dictatorship. I can't take over. In the first place, Boggs would probably object a lot, and the only way I could take the schooner away from him would be sort of violent. In the second place, even if I could do it without hurting him, and the rest of you all cheered me on, it would still be mutiny. This schooner is on a mission for the British government. The British government hangs mutineers. Those are the rules of the game."

"Pooh, some rules are made to be broken."

He said, "Mutiny's not one I break lightly. But, yeah, I can bend some of Queen Vickie's sillier rules."

She gasped, "What's that hand doing on my breast, sir?"

He pinched her turgid nipple between his cupping fingers and thumb as he grinned at her and answered, "Just breaking a few rules. Chester sure is a good name for you, bubbles."

She dimpled but insisted, "Take your hand away from there at once!"

He lay back across the bed with her and did as she asked. He slid his free hand off her voluptuous breast to slide it down and inside her kimono on the way to greater glory. Her conversational talents weren't half as interesting as the naked curves under the smooth silk, so to shut her up he kissed her. It was probably a relief to her as well, not to have to make up words a lady was expected to say at times like these. For she kissed and tongued him back like a greedy child devouring sweets, and although she stiffened and made a half-baked attempt to cross her creamy thighs when he cupped her mons in his hand, she stopped her feeble struggles and spread her legs as soon as he began to finger her.

As he'd expected, she was already well lubricated down there, and his own privates were ready for action, too. So he simply let the pillow in his lap roll any old place it wanted to as he proceeded to mount her.

When he had to stop kissing her for a moment as he rolled in place atop her, she whimpered, "Please, sir, I'm not that kind of girl."

But by then he had her with her derriere braced on the edge of the mattress, with his bare feet braced on the deck and his hips between her open legs. So he said, "You are, now," and thrust home to the roots as Phoebe gasped in pleasured surprise.

She said, "Oh, my God, it's too big. You're abso-bloody-lutely splitting me with that perishing great tool!" But even as she protested, Phoebe was loosening the sash of her kimono to let the blue silk fall away to either side as their bare torsos combined forces. As he flattened her heroic tits against his chest and kissed her hard again, Phoebe was unable to protest further, so, what the hell, she started screwing like a mink.

She raised her knees and enveloped his naked body in her arms and legs as she thrust hard to meet him with her pelvis and gasped the shaft inside her with muscular skill that hinted at lots of practice. He didn't mind. He'd had a lot of practice too, and she wasn't the sort of girl a guy thought about taking home to mother. She was clean, beautiful, a fantastic lay, and at best a moron. In other words, exactly the kind of girl a hard-up guy thinks about when he's jerking off. So, after he'd ejaculated in her the old-fashioned way, Captain Gringo got her up on the bunk on her hands and knees to enjoy an innocent sex fantasy or two with her.

It was more than two. Phoebe wasn't bright about most things. But she was blessed with a vivid imagination when it came to sex. Aside from taking shorthand, another art that takes more skill than brains, Phoebe concentrated all her physical and mental skills on the art in which she was most skilled. Once the ice had been broken and even she could see that it was a little dumb to go on protesting innocence, Phoebe made love like an experienced, expensive whore showing off to a pal. She offered to take it all three ways, so she got to. Her greedy little mouth and rectal muscles were amazingly skilled, too. So Captain Gringo wasn't keeping track of her orgasms at first. But when they finally took a break and he lay back, sated, with Phoebe's blond head on his shoulder and her hand fondling his semi-erection, he asked her casually, "How many times did you get there, honey? You didn't mention coming, at the time."

She toyed with his shaft teasingly as she answered, "Oh, I never come."

"You don't?" He frowned, adding, "How come you seem to enjoy it so much, then? You sure as hell don't *act* frigid, Phoebe!"

"Pooh, I'm not frigid. I love to make love. It feels bloody marvelous."

"I noticed. But, no shit, don't you *ever* come?"

She sighed and answered, "I don't even know what it's supposed to feel like. I've been told I'm missing something grand. I've tried making something happen by using my fingers and even, well, wax bananas and so forth. A doctor I consulted said I was a classic nymphomaniac."

"That sounds reasonable. But what did the doc tell you about the way you can screw by the hour without, ah, results?"

"He said that was why I was a nymphomaniac. Girls

who have easy orgasms tend to want to stop. Isn't it grand that I don't have to? I love to play with perishing great dongs, and I get to do it hour after hour!"

Captain Gringo laughed and said, "It sounds a little frightening. I've read that some famous, ah, sporting gals didn't really enjoy sex, but . . ."

"Oh, no, Dick," she cut in, "I love sex! Now that we're such friends, I may as well confess I was hoping you'd seduce me when I came in here. I knew you had a great dong, and . . . Hmm, speaking of great dongs, this one's beginning to show signs of life again."

He felt the renewed throbbing in his shaft as she skillfully played with it. But he was still more curious than desperate, so he asked, "Seriously now, Phoebe. What's the point of all this for you? I'm okay for the moment and you don't get anything out of it, so what are we out to prove?"

She looked up at him in innocent wonder and asked, "Do we have to prove something darling? Fucking is *fun!*"

"Yeah, but if you don't come . . ."

"Pooh, don't you enjoy it *before* you come?"

"Well, sure, it feels fantastic, just going in, but . . . Hmm, I'm starting to see the light. Girls like you get all the pleasure leading up to the climax, and just miss the climax, right? It must be sort of like enjoying a good novel and not getting to read the end."

"Haven't you ever found yourself reading a book so good you hoped it would never end?"

"Yeah, I said I got the point, odd as it sounds. And speaking of points . . ."

"Yes, it does seem hard enough now." She giggled, pulled away to get on her hands and knees above him, then lowered herself onto his lap. She hissed in pleasure as she spitted herself on his shaft, saying, "My God, that feels yummy. I'm so happy you're not as, well, short-winded as some chaps I've met."

As she started moving up and down, he laughed and said, "So am I. I've heard it's a greater joy to give than to receive, but you give indeed, and if I hadn't started out hard up, you'd have finished me off by now!"

She shot a worried look down at him as she moved faster, her big breasts bouncing out of gait with her rippling belly muscles as she pleaded, "You don't mean to quit on me so soon, do you?"

He arched his spine to thrust deeper as she did most of the work. He laughed and said, "I think I'm game for another round. But, ah, how do we know when *you've* had enough, Phoebe?"

"I never get enough. Alas, I generally stop when the gentleman I'm with forces me to by falling bloody asleep!"

So the tall, muscular American relaxed and enjoyed it, as well as a man could enjoy a beautiful, not-too-bright sex freak. One part of his mind was somewhat miffed that she wasn't fully enjoying his body as much as he was enjoying hers. On the other hand, it sure beat masturbation, and there were things to be said for making it with a frigid but willing partner. He didn't have to concern himself with pleasing her. Knowing it wasn't possible, he could just let himself go in her anytime he wanted to and not feel like a selfish heel. Phoebe offered all the carefree joys of a beautiful, clean whore, without the distaste a man felt for having to pay and probably seeming foolish to a woman who had no respect for him. Phoebe obviously didn't think of him as a john. Hell, she didn't think at all. So what was he thinking so much about? He was in bed with a beautiful dame and hard as a rock, now. What else was there to know?

He rolled her over, keeping it in her as they exchanged positions of dominance. As he began to pound her in innocent selfishness, the little but pneumatic blonde sighed. "Oh, loverly! Can you rub it harder against the bottom, dear? I like to make dongs hard. It makes me feel good when I know I've made a man as hard as he can bloody get!"

He didn't answer. Her ideas were too weird to talk about. Phoebe seemed arrested in some immature stage where sex organs were confused in her mind with toys, and, for Chrissake, she was playing *dolls* with his old organ grinder!

He found himself slowing down. The stateroom was like a steam bath, and they were both filmed with sweat as their flesh slid against each other's. Her bubbly body was still stimulating him, but her bubbly mind, and the odd things she had in it, were throwing him off his feed a bit. He'd lost count of how many times he'd ejaculated in her, or where, and although it still felt great to slide in and out of her, it was starting to feel more like work than passion. He moved them into an easier position for him, with him semi-reclining on his side, with one of Phoebe's drawn-up knees pillowing his ribs as he rutted with her sideways. She protested, "It doesn't go as deep that way." So he put his free hand down between them to massage her moist, wet clit as he slid his shaft in and out just under it. She giggled and said, "That tickles. Why are you playing with that little bump I have there?"

"Don't you? It's supposed to feel good to girls, Phoebe."

"It does. But what do you mean, don't I? It's just a perishing bump."

Her clit was responding to his fingering as he frowned and said, "You told me you'd played with yourself without results, doll. Do you mean to tell me you never stroked your own clit?"

"Is that what you call it? I thought it was just another fold. Why should I want to muck about with my pussy trimmings, Dick? I thought the idea was to fill the real thing up as often and as much as possible."

He muttered, "I don't believe this." But he didn't try to explain. There was still a chance her clit was as frigid as everything else, if one could call her lovely, pulsing vagina frigid. He started timing his thrusts with the movement of his hand as Phoebe spread her thighs wider and lay her head back to sigh, "Oh, that does feel yummy. Both places are starting to feel so . . . so bloody fucked!"

Her hip movements and the way her innocent clit was starting to swell inspired him to greater effort, and if he wasn't breaking in a virgin in a grotesque way indeed, it was still a lot of fun to try.

He was. Phoebe's internal muscles began to pulsate wildly as she rolled her blond head from side to side and moaned, "Oh, stop! Something mad is happening! I fear we did it too much today after all and I'm starting to feel faint and . . . Oh, my God, what you *doing* to me?"

He didn't answer in words. He rolled deeper into the saddle and began to pound her deep and hard as he kept massaging her excited, albeit innocent, clit. Phoebe suddenly cried, "Oh, Jesus, stop! You're driving me mad! I think I'm going to piss or something. It feels so strange. It feels so . . . oh, bloody *marvelous!*"

He liked it, too. As she contracted in a prolonged, shuddering orgasm around his shaft, he let go of her other pleasure center and let himself go completely, topping off her first orgasm with an old-fashioned pounding. He ejaculated in her. It felt so good he kept going. It felt good to her, too, for she dug her nails into his buttocks as she tried to take him, balls and all, moaning. "Oh, sweet Jesus, it's happening again!" And so it did, for both of them.

As they relaxed, later, sharing smoke and cuddles, Phoebe murmured, "So that's what it feels like to come. I was wondering what all the fuss was about."

"Are you sorry, Phoebe?"

"Pooh, not bloody likely. I've never felt such a thrill in my life." Then she took a drag on his cigar, handed it back to him, and added with a little sigh, "At least, I don't think I'm sorry. You've opened some new horizons indeed for me, darling. But I'm not sure I'll ever be the same girl again. I mean, somehow I feel, well, relaxed down there now. I see now why most people can fall asleep when it's over. I fear now I'll never be able to go on as long with a bloke."

"Look, there's quantity and there's quality. I'm not sure you'd better fall asleep right now, though. It's still broad day out and Gaston could pop in on us any minute."

She laughed and said, "Up until a few moments ago I might have suggested he join us for a game of three in a boat. But you're right—for the first time since I learned to screw, I seem to have had enough for now."

As she sat up to slip on her kimono, Phoebe sighed and added, "God damn you, Dick Walker. I fear you may have ruined me as a sexual athlete!"

They made Corozal after nightfall, so Captain Boggs thought they were slipping into the harbor pretty slickly. Anyone who knew the tropics could have told Boggs that the tropic natives tend to be night people and that everyone would be up, bright-eyed and bushy-tailed, looking for excitement after the dull, hot afternoon siesta. Captain Gringo knew the tropics better than he wanted to, but he didn't say anything to Boggs as the *Flamenco Lass* steamed in with sails furled, lest someone mistake them for poor fisher folk.

Corozal lay between the estuaries of the New River to the south and the Hondo to the north. The Hondo was the border between British Honduras and Los Estados

Unidos de Mexico, according to the British. The Mexicans had other ideas. Guatemala, to the west, inland, claimed the same land. The British had simply moved in and set up shop all along the Mosquito Coast earlier in the century. Later, they'd given most of the Nicaraguan part of the coast to Nicaragua, which had no doubt pleased the Nicaraguans, but tended to make others feel that if they pushed hard enough they could have the rest. And British Honduras was about it. Thus, in addition to Spanish agents one could worry about, Corozal offered endless possibilities for Mexican, Guatemalan, and U.S. agents, now that President Cleveland was on the prod about the Monroe Doctrine and the recent flap he'd had with Her Majesty to the south in Venezuela.

A customs launch came out to meet *Flamenco Lass*. They went away after Boggs showed them papers indicating that he was on Her Majesty's business, of course. Captain Gringo thought it was a swell move. The black enlisted men manning the customs launch would be going off duty any minute, and of course they wouldn't say a word in any waterfront cantina, right?

They tied up in the basin of the Royal Yacht Club. Where else? And Boggs went ashore to see about arranging for the burial of the dead crew member, now reposed under canvas in the hopefully cooler hold.

Lieutenant Carmichael and one of his diving crew approached Captain Gringo on deck as soon as Boggs had left. Carmichael said, "Your chum, the Frenchman, says you chaps know this port, Walker."

Captain Gringo nodded and replied, "We got shot at the last time we were here. This is the first time I've ever been to the Royal Yacht Club. Guys in my line of work generally hide out in darker corners."

Carmichael said, "I agree Boggs is a bloody ass. What are we going to do about it, Walker?"

"Beats the shit out of me. This is sort of a public place

to stage a mutiny. That gray lump over to the south isn't a whale gazing at the moon. It's a Royal Navy torpedo ram. I noticed it the last time we were here."

Carmichael nodded and said, "Mutiny is out of the question, even if it were possible. But there must be a telegraph office here in Corozal, and you seem to have some influence with Mr. Greystoke."

"Not that much. You were there when I told him I thought the whole plan was for the birds. Did he listen? Greystoke picked Boggs to sail us to wherever. So he'd be admitting a mistake if he fired Boggs. I've never heard Greystoke admit he wasn't beautiful, let alone admit a mistake. How do you guys feel about desertion?"

"Desertion? You can't be serious! That's as bad as mutiny!"

"I thought you'd say that. Look, guys, I don't know what you and the others can do, legally."

"What are you and Verrier going to do, Walker?"

"We're still thinking about it," the tall American replied, moving away as he added. "You're spinning your wheels on the track, Carmichael. In a situation like this, it's best not to stand around plotting unless somebody has a sensible plot. There's always a captain's pet in every crew, and it's dumb to have the name without the game."

He moved along the seaward rail, as if it mattered whether anyone was watching from shore at this range. He spotted Gaston lounging amidships against the cabin works. As he moved to join him, Gaston put a finger to his lips and pointed at a familiar ventilator.

Captain Gringo nodded and hooked his rump over the low rooftop to listen, too, as Phoebe's voice said hollowly, "I was so surprised I nearly farted on the poor dear's balls!"

Captain Gringo knew they were talking about him when Flora Manson answered wearily, "Good God, Phoebe, don't you ever think about anything but sex? I told you

I wasn't interested in your manic career as this century's answer to Cleopatra. Why can't you just fornicate to your heart's content and keep it to yourself?"

"Pooh, I keep an awful lot of things I do to myself. But this afternoon was so bloody unusual. You'll never believe what he did to me, Flora!"

"Oh, for God's sake, you know I used to be married, Phoebe. What on earth can any man do that every married woman hasn't tried at least once?"

"He made me *come!* Can you believe that?"

There was a moment of stunned silence. Then Flora said, "Oh? I'm missing something, Phoebe. What's so bloody unusual about that? Isn't that what one sneaks about in kimonos to accomplish, as a rule?"

"Well, God knows I've tried to come often enough, Flora. But this afternoon was the first time I ever managed. And I came *twice!*"

Another silence, followed by, "I suspected that might have been why you acted so man-hungry. All right, welcome to the club. Obviously Captain Gringo knows his business, and I'm happy for you. Can we get some sleep now? Captain Boggs says he means to bury that poor lad at dawn, and it's getting late."

There was another interval of silence, so Captain Gringo nudged Gaston and motioned him away. But Gaston shook his head and whispered, "I find this *trés intrigue,* you devil!"

Captain Gringo muttered a curse and lit a smoke in time to hear Phoebe say, "I do feel ever so much more relaxed tonight. But I wish he was here right now to put me to sleep proper with his great dong."

Flora snapped, "Will you shut up, you silly little slut!"

"What's the matter? Did I say something wrong, dear?"

"Oh, for God's sake, go to sleep."

There was a longer-than-ever lull. Captain Gringo whispered, "Can we go now? I want to talk to you."

Gaston shook his head and in a little while they heard Phoebe giggle and say, "Oh, I know why you're so cross with me. You haven't come in ages and you don't feel as comfy as me, eh what?"

Flora's voice dripped honey and venom as she said, "To feel like you I'd doubtless have to scoop out my brains and toss them away. But, for the record, it's not polite to prattle on about one's sex life to someone who doesn't have one."

"Oh, are you hard up, Flora? Why don't I fix it up for you to get to come too? Dick says he shares that stateroom with that nice little French chap, and . . ."

"Now you're really starting to disgust me, Phoebe! In the first place, I don't want to have an affair with anyone, but, if I did, M'sieur Verrier is old enough to be my father!"

"Well, he's sort of cute, though. I'll tell you what. Why don't I fix it up so that you can sleep with Dick and I can try my newfound interests with Gaston? I wonder if it's true what they say about Frenchmen. Now that I know what it feels like to come, the idea of a tongue down there just makes me shiver all over!"

They heard a strangled curse and the slamming of a cabin door. Captain Gringo bodily pulled Gaston away as he said, "Come on. She may come on deck to cool off, and that Phoebe never shuts up, even when she's alone."

As he led Gaston forward, the Frenchman laughed and said, "I tingle, too. You seem to have created a monster, Dick. But I admire her sense of adventure very much."

"You can have her. Kiss it once for me for old times' sake. That's not what I wanted to talk to you about. Take a gander at that other schooner, moored out in the roads to the northeast."

Gaston followed his gaze and stared for a time at the dim outlines of a nondescript coastal schooner, blacked out and silent at anchor. Gaston shrugged and said, *"Eh bien,* it is a boat. So what?"

"I think it could be the *Nombre Nada.* Remember her?"

"Mes, oui, we are discussing the gunrunner owned by that rather ferocious Esperanza, who also admired your great dong so much, *non?"*

"Old Esperanza and I get along okay. That's not the point. Finding a dame in Corozal isn't much of a problem. Finding a dame with a seagoing schooner is the problem. If that schooner is the *Nombre Nada,* things are looking up, old buddy! Esperanza owes me. I did more than make her come the last time we met. I saved her life and schooner, remember?"

"Ah, I follow your drift, as *les* cowboys say. But how are we to know that is the *Nombre Nada* over there, and, more important, how are we to get aboard, unseen, if she is?"

"I'm still working on that. The first thing we have to find out is if Esperanza is in town and where her next port of call might be. I'm tired of jumping from the frying pan into the fire, and Esperanza runs guns to some weird places for a living."

Gaston placed a forefinger against his nose and said, "You stay here. A big blond moose like you attracts attention, even in a British tropic port. I, sneaky Gaston, shall slip ashore and make discreet inquiries among the rogues of Corozal." He looked wistfully back at the vent they'd left and added, "I may have to search out a lady rogue as well. That mad little English girl has given me an astounding erection for a man my age."

Gaston got back before midnight, which surprised Captain Gringo almost as much as it did Gaston. They met near the gangplank. Gaston asked, "*Sacrebleu,* what are you doing with your pants on at this hour, standing guard on this *très fatigue* deck?"

Captain Gringo said, "I'm not. There's a lime juicer on watch in the cockpit. I was waiting for Boggs to get back. I wasn't expecting you before morning."

"Neither was I, alas. But all the rogues I was able to contact turned out to be male rogues. Do you remember that retired daughter of joy I spent some time with the last time we were here? They tell me she has been deported by the spoilsport constabulary, just for stabbing an annoying guest. Corozal used to be a more interesting port of call, but . . ."

"Never mind all that. What did you find out about that blacked-out schooner over there?"

"She is still the *Nombre Nada* to the extent that she has no known name to anyone I met on the beach. Whether she is Esperanza's *Nombre Nada* or not is another matter. Nobody seems to know who is aboard or what they are up to in Corozal. Frankly, that sounds like Esperanza to me. She is a rogue after my own heart, even though she seems to prefer you in bed. If that mystery schooner was not a gunrunner, she would not be keeping her business here so quiet, *non?* After all, the rogues on shore know all about *this* vessel and it's crew."

Captain Gringo blinked and said, "Run that by me again. Are you saying our cover's been blown?"

"But of course. What did you expect would happen when that species of idiot, Boggs, went ashore to ask directions to an Anglican High Church chapel where he could hold a funeral for a crew member killed by gunfire? Naturally, the tavern gossips do not have the whole story in detail. But they know *Flamenco Lass* is on some sort of mission of derring-do for the British government. You were right that the enlisted men aboard that customs craft would comment over supper about our mysterious immunity from standard procedure, and anyone with the brain of a flea can put two and two together, *hein?*"

Captain Gringo muttered, "Shit. Okay, what I figured would happen has happened, and a knock-around guy has to roll with the punches."

"Can we desert now, Dick?"

"No. We're safer here than anywhere I can think of for the moment. Boggs won't want to shove off for at least eight or nine hours. Come daybreak, we can see if we can find out how many old pals we may have here in port. Why don't you turn in? I'll wait here for Boggs. I know it's a waste of time, but I still want to tell him he's an asshole."

Gaston laughed and went below. Captain Gringo finished his smoke, decided not to light another just yet, and paced the deck as he waited for Boggs to return. It was a long wait and he was getting bored. But he didn't go back to the cockpit to chat with the deck watch. The sailor was a morose Welshman named Rice, who answered in sullen grunts, and the Yank wasn't interested in what was eating him.

Boggs finally arrived at about quarter to one. He seemed pleased with himself as he told Captain Gringo that the funeral was set for nine o'clock that morning and added, "Entire ship's complement to be present and suitably dressed, of course."

Captain Gringo said, "Bad move. Any kind of funeral is going to attract more attention than we really need. Follow the pall with men in uniform and two white women gussied to the nines and we'll make the front page of the local newspaper. Besides, at least half of us should stay aboard to guard the vessel."

"Nonsense. What could happen to it here in the yacht-club basin? I'll leave a skeleton crew aboard, of course. That's regulation."

"Good. Gaston and I volunteer to stay here. Neither

of us owns a necktie, and I'd feel silly as hell if somebody stole my weapons."

Bogg answered with a shrug that probably meant yes. So Captain Gringo pressed his luck and added, "I'd like the use of your captain's gig, as soon as the sun comes up, to shed more light on the subject. I want to go over and have a closer look at another tub in the harbor."

"We're not supposed to communicate with anyone else about our mission, Walker."

Captain Gringo swallowed what he was hurting to point out and contented himself with explaining, in a reasonable tone, "The people I'm hoping to meet are sort of in the same trade, as freelancers, of course. I can vouch for them as knock-around types who stay bought. I worked with them in the past on another mission, and they owe me."

· "Oh? Was it a mission for the British government?"

"No. Just gun-for-hire stuff. But old Esperanza and her crew could come in handy if I could get them to join forces with us. They know every pirate cove and corrupt official on the Mosquito Coast."

Boggs shook his head and said, "Out of the question. Whitehall would never approve of our enlisting amateurs."

"Jesus H. Christ! You call Esperanza and her gun-runners *amateurs*? They're professional sneaks, hard as nails, and, like I said, they know this coast better than you, me, Greystoke, and even Gaston put together!"

Boggs shook his head again and said, "They're still amateurs, or, if you wish, irregulars, as far as Whitehall is concerned. I don't want to talk to them, and I don't want you to talk to them. Will that be all? I'd like to go to my quarters, if you don't mind."

Captain Gringo wished him pleasant dreams about the bunny rabbits and, since Boggs was turning in, decided to do the same.

He went below and opened the door to the stateroom

he shared with Gaston. Gaston was not alone. Phoebe Chester gleeped, "Oh, dear!" as Captain Gringo entered. She had a right to feel embarrassed. She was reclining, naked, on Gaston's bunk. Gaston should have felt embarrassed, too, but he just went on eating her between the legs. So Captain Gringo muttered, "Sorry," and stepped over to his own bunk to scoop up his mattress and bedding.

As he turned to go, Phoebe giggled and said, "Don't leave, Dick. I know this may look naughty, but I like you both, and if you'd like to stay and have a part . . ."

He didn't answer. He just closed the door softly behind him. He was maybe a little pissed, but a wise older woman had once told him that no parting words topped gently closing the door behind you as you simply left, and he'd found that to be, if not true, a lot less effort than any other parting shots one could come up with on short notice.

He grumped his way back up on deck and moved forward. That flat expanse up in the bows offered as good a place as any to spread his bedding and kip out. It didn't look like rain, and the night air tasted fresher in the open, anyway.

When he got up in the bows, he discovered that someone else had already had the same idea. Flora Manson gasped and asked, "What are you doing here?" as she rose on one elbow under her sheet and thin coverlet. In the moonlight he could see she was in her black lace nightgown, and that looked sort of thin, too.

He began to spread his own bedding a foot or more from Flora's as he explained, "My stateroom's a bit crowded as well as stuffy at the moment. Mind if I join you?"

"I certainly do! You can't sleep with me, you idiot!"

"Hey, there's sleeping with and then there's sleeping beside, right? Look, I know you were here first, but I have

55

no choice. I've got no place else to kip out. What's the matter with your own stateroom, if you don't trust me? I happened to know it's empty right now."

As he sat down and took off his gun rig and boots, intending to leave the rest of his duds on, for now, Flora frowned and said, "I know my stateroom is empty. My roommate told me she was on her way to yours."

He laughed and said, "She told you true. That's why I came up here." Then he got under his own covers, lay back, and added, "Pleasant dreams."

There was an interval of silence as they lay side by side, staring up at the tropic stars through the rigging. Then Flora sat up again and said, "This is all very confusing. What on earth is Phoebe doing in your bunk if you're up here with me?"

He chuckled and said, "She wasn't in my bunk, last time I looked. I'm too much a gent to tell you what she was doing. But it seemed to be a private matter, so I thought I'd better leave."

"Oh, my God, not Phoebe and that dirty old man!"

"I didn't notice how dirty anybody was. The light was sort of dim. But let's not be calling my pal names, eh? He may be older than you and me, but he's not doing anything to Phoebe that Phoebe doesn't want him to."

Flora grimaced and said, "You're right. I shouldn't have made that uncalled-for remark about your friend. I know what you men are like, and Phoebe seems a perfect perishing little slut!"

He shrugged and opined, "That's her business, not ours. I don't like to hang labels on people. What people might or might not be depends on who's looking at them. To a nun, a respectable married woman may appear sexually depraved. A salmon swimming up a river would probably think all of us were acting silly, if a salmon knew how we spawned."

Flora laughed despite herself and said, "What a grotesque idea! How on earth can you even guess what a salmon feels about, ah, country matters?"

"I can't. I've never been a salmon. I know his sex life seems a little weird to me. But, like I said, it's all in one's point of view. As long as other people aren't trying to make you do something you don't want to, I figure they have a right to their own opinions. Can we drop it? I'm trying to be a gent, but I'm not used to discussing sex with beautiful women at bedtime, unless I know them pretty well."

They both fell silent again. It wasn't easy. Despite himself, Captain Gringo was aware that there was a lush brunette, naked under black lace, less than a yard away, and how in hell was he supposed to fall asleep with an erection like this?

Flora must have had feelings, too, although she had a piss-poor way of coping with them. She suddenly blurted, "Do you really think I'm pretty?"

"I didn't say you were pretty. I said you were beautiful. Now, if you don't want me to do anything about it, go to sleep, for chrissake!"

She didn't. She asked, "Did you enjoy making love to Phoebe?"

He sighed and said, "That's a stupid question. You know that if I had, I wouldn't tell you. A gent's not supposed to kiss and tell."

She repressed a laugh and said, "You don't have to. Phoebe already told me you did much more than kiss her."

He didn't answer. He didn't want to let her know he'd been listening in on the conversation. He also knew there were times when silence was golden. He was hoping like hell that this was one of them. Damn, those tits looked nice in the moonlight under black lace!

She tried to hold out, too. Then she tried, "Do you mean to tell me Phoebe just made that up about you making her, ah, you know?"

"How the hell should I know anything, if she made it up?"

"Something must have happened. She came back from your stateroom absolutely radiant."

"Look, what's the point of all this, Flora? I'm not on trial. I don't owe you any explanations. I don't give a damn what you think might have happened between Phoebe and me. You can think anything you like. What difference does it make if she indulged in some harmless boasting or if I painted her blue and flew to the moon with her?"

Flora sighed and said, "I'd like to think she just made it up. But I suppose you must have gone all the way with her."

"Yeah? What makes you so sure? Do you peek through keyholes a lot?"

She giggled wistfully and said, "I said you men are all alike. If you hadn't been, well, satisfied with yourself when you found me here alone in bed, you'd have doubtless made a pass at me."

That did it. He sat up, threw his covers off, and slid over to her as he said, "Hell, if the only way I can prove my innocence is to display some virility . . ."

But she flinched away and pleaded, "Don't, Dick! Please don't. I didn't mean it that way at all!"

Sure she didn't. But, as it turned out, her protestations were academic. For just as Captain Gringo was reaching for her covers, all hell broke loose!

A long, ragged burst of machine-gun fire, mingled with the thudding of hot lead into the timbers of *Flamenco Lass,* flattened Captain Gringo atop Flora Manson as she screamed. But he was only shielding her body with his own as a blacked-out powered launch sped past them into the darkness, still spitting lead from the machine gun mounted on its rail. As he saw what in hell was going on, Captain Gringo snapped, "Stay down!" and rolled off Flora to grope for his gun rig on the deck and draw his double-action .38. He didn't aim it at the vanishing mystery craft. It was out of range and had ceased fire, too. He just felt more comfortable with a gun in his fist as he ran aft to check the damage.

The survivors helped, of course, and the news was good and bad. The machine gunner in the launch had stitched a line of bullet holes along the seaward side of *Flamenco Lass* from stern to stem. Fortunately for the schooner, above the waterline. Fortunately for Captain Gringo and the girl in the bows, below the rail. They'd been aiming at the ports along the schooner's side. So, below decks, things were messier.

The stateroom shared by the two girls had been shot to shit, and the air was filled with floating feathers from their exploded empty bunks, proving that virtue does not always offer its own reward.

The gear in the main salon had been protected by food cases, and, save for beans and bully beeef spattered all over, there was no serious damage.

One of Carmichael's diving assistants lay dead in his shot-up bunk, staring blankly at the blood-spattered ceiling. When Captain Gringo failed to notice Boggs among the milling survivors in various stages of dishabille, he told Phoebe, for chrissake, to put some duds on, then went to Boggs's stateroom.

Boggs lay face down on the floor, covered with blood and mattress feathers. One didn't have to turn him over to know he was dead. Boggs wasn't going anywhere important, either. So Captain Gringo shut the door and assembled everyone in the main salon, where he said, "Okay, gang, you all know somebody's mad at us. With Boggs dead, we're playing by new rules. Up front, I'm taking command. Does anybody want to make something of it?"

The Welshman, Rice, said, "I do, look you! Who made you our C.O., Yank?"

So Captain Gringo flattened him with a left cross, kicked him the rest of the way to dreamland with his bare foot, and said, "I did. Does anyone else have any objections?"

No answer.

He nodded grimly and said, "Okay. We're pressed for time. You, you, and you, start cleaning up the mess. Put all the bodies in the hold for now. I have to get up on deck before the town law boards us to ask all sorts of dumb questions. Gaston, get your gun and your pants and come with me. You there with the mustache, pour some water over Rice and tell him he has the rest of the watch off."

He and Gaston, along with Carmichael, made it to the deck in time. Just. A couple of black constables in white uniforms were approaching the shoreward end of the gangplank.

Captain Gringo waved down to them and called out, "What can I do for you, chaps?"

The senior constable called back, "We heard shots, sir. A lot of shots, just now. They seemed to be coming from somewhere hereabouts."

Captain Gringo said, "We heard them, too. Sounded like a machine gun. It was somebody out on the water. I'm afraid that's all we know."

"Permission to come aboard, sir?"

Carmichael stiffened. But Gaston gripped his arm warningly as Captain Gringo answered, "Permission granted. You have my word nobdy aboard this vessel fired any shots. But you're welcome to look about if you like."

The two blacks consulted with each other in low voices. Then the one in charge laughed and said, "There's no need to trouble you, sir. We can see you all are sober gentlefolk, and we've a lot of ground to cover."

"Sure you don't want to come aboard for a drink?"

"Thank you, sir. We're not allowed to do that. Goodnight to you, sir."

As the two white-clad constables moved down the dock and out of earshot, Carmichael let out a wheeze and said, "Coo, I thought we were sunk for a mo, there!"

Gaston chuckled and said, "Mes non, it was those policemen who were in danger, not us. Our sneaky young friend here knows how to deal with suspicious officials."

Carmichael asked Captain Gringo, "Would you have?"

The American just smiled crookedly and answered, "Since they didn't come aboard, we'll never know. I was hoping they wouldn't bother, once it seemed we didn't mind. Never tell a cop he can't come in, Carmichael. It's the surest way to get him to at least try."

He struck a match to light a smoke before he added, "Okay. We seem to be safe for the moment. But by now even Boggs would have figured out we're in trouble, if the trouble hadn't killed him. We've been unmasked by the other side. Worse yet, we don't know who in hell the other side is. We're going to have to abort the mission, or make some shifty moves indeed in the next few hours. So let's get cracking."

By sunrise Captain Gringo had thought up a dozen sneaky ways to find out who was aboard that mysterious, nondescript schooner anchored farther out in the harbor. But none of them sounded easier or better than simply rowing over in the captain's gig and asking. When Gaston pointed out that the machine-gun attack might well have originated from other quarters, Captain Gringo said, "So what? Who's going to open fire on us in broad daylight in sight of a British torpedo ram? That schooner may or may not have auxiliary power. But she's not about to out-run Royal Navy shells, and the ram will put one across her bows if she tries to up anchor and leave before ex-plaining her noisy habits."

Gaston shrugged and replied, "True. But what if they let us aboard and then grab us, Dick?"

"That's why I'm going aboard and you're not. If I'm grabbed, you row over and tell teacher. It'll blow the mission for sure, but the Royal Navy's not about to let anyone leave the harbor wtih a kidnap victim aboard, either."

"Are you forgetting you're a wanted outlaw, or that Britain has an extradition treaty with *les* States, Dick?"

"I hadn't forgotten. But I wish you hadn't reminded me. You eat the apple a bite at a time, Gaston. The first bite is to identify that schooner over there, so let's do it."

So they did. Leaving Carmichael in command, Captain Gringo took Gaston and four oarsmen to row out to the mystery schooner. As they approached, figures began to appear on deck. Captain Gringo spotted one in a yellow oilskin and grinned. He said, "We're in luck. Nobody else is built like Esperanza!"

The big brunette in the slicker recognized Captain Gringo's tall blond form at about the same time and waved. Gaston said, *"Eh bien,* as she raised the arm to pull tight the oilcloth, one observes the heroic tits. But why the slicker in the first place? The sky is clear and the sun is rising hot and dry."

Captain Gringo said, "She sleeps in the buff, and she must have been awakened by her deck watch when they spotted us. It only takes a second to slip on oilskins, right?"

"You mean she's naked under that yellow slicker? Ah, but why do I ask such foolish questions. Everyone knows she is a sex maniac."

Aware that others were listening, Captain Gringo muttered, "Watch it. I know for a fact Esperanza doesn't mess around with her crew."

"Ah, bad for discipline, *non?* But you are not a member of her crew, you lucky devil. One takes it there will be no need for us to wait for you in this hot sun?"

"Let's cross our bridges when we come to them. It's the lady's tub, and it's been a while. Let's make for that sea ladder, guys."

The captain's gig bumped against the rungs of the sea ladder down the side of *Nombre Nada,* and Captain Gringo leaped lightly onto it and hauled himself up to the deck. There he was greeted by the schooner's mistress, Esperanza, who would have felt flattered to be described as one big tough broad who'd have not only been right at home in a Cro-Magnon cave but probably would have run the tribe. Esperanza was capable of beating to death or screwing to death the average man, depending on how she felt about him. She extended her hand to Captain Gringo and said gravely, *"Mi casa es su casa,* Deek. It has been a long time."

Actually, it had been only a few months. But as they faced each other, knowingly, Captain Gringo felt sorry that he'd been away so long. Aside from being big and tough, Esperanza was beautiful. Her Castilian features were delicately flavored with Spanish Basque and Spanish gypsy genes. Her complexion was that odd shade of ripe peach found only among white Hispanics. Her beautiful face was softened by a frame of wavy midnight-black hair, parted at the widow's peak above her brow. In truth, it needed a little softening. Esperanza's brows were heavier than most women's, and her jaw was bigger and firmer than that of a fashionable Gibson Girl. The other crew members hung back discreetly as Esperanza held on to his hand and said, "Let us go to my cabin where we can be more comfortable, eh?"

"Should I have my gig wait, Esperanza?"

"You know better than that, Deek. My own *muchachos* can row you back, if you ever mean to leave me again, you cruel thing."

So Captain Gringo waved his transportation off and went with Esperanza to her cabin. Like Esperanza herself, the cabin was plush and a little musky. Her earthly odor of perfume and honest sweat would have been less enticing had he not known that she didn't screw around with her crew. She'd doubtless been in bed with a dozen guys since the last time they'd met. But what the hell, he'd been taking baths between women, too.

He started to explain his visit. But Esperanza had already locked the door and slipped out of her yellow slicker. So he knew she wasn't in a conversational mood. He took her in his arms and kissed her. Then he picked her up and carried her over to the wide, soft bunk.

Captain Gringo had never been married, and a guy in his line of work didn't get to shack up for very long at a time. But there was something to be said for getting into bed with familiar flesh. Esperanza lay back dreamily as he sat beside her and undressed in silence. There was no need for words. They understood each other. He simply dropped his duds to the floor and rolled aboard her like an old friend.

Captain Gringo hissed, "Oh, yesss!" as he entered her lush, dank depths.

Esperanza wrapped her muscular arms around him but spread her big thighs as wide as they would go as she murmured, "Welcome home, *querido*."

Then they both went pleasantly crazy for a while. As they'd discovered in the past, their bodies meshed perfectly without effort, and each knew how to move without asking. Esperanza was an uncomplicated earth mother who had no problems with sex and climaxed easily and often. As he ejaculated in her and kept going, Captain Gringo was glad he hadn't scored with Flora after all last night. At the time, he'd been mad as hell at that machine gunner for busting up his budding romance. But even a man as virile as Captain Gringo needed to save up for Esperanza.

Unlike the confused Phoebe Chester, Esperanza was not a nymphomaniac. She simply liked to screw. She enjoyed it as naturally as if she were a man. So, after they'd climaxed together a few times, she was content to take a breather and nestled comfortably against him as he lay propped on her pillows and lit a smoke. She said, "That was lovely. I was hoping you were in port when I heard that machine gun going off last night, Deek. Was that you?"

He said, "No. I was hoping you might know who it was. I'm working for the Brits on a sneaky-sneaky up the coast. We're aboard that sharp-looking schooner in the yacht basin."

"I noticed it. It has beautiful lines. Is it fast?"

"Not fast enough to outsail a gunboat shell. Unfortunately, somebody we don't know seems to have made us out. What are you guys doing here in Corozal, Esperanza?"

She cuddled closer and sighed. "Hiding out. We are being hunted, too. I've contracted to deliver certain industrial products in my hold to the Panamanian rebels. Some damned informer tipped off the Colombian navy. I never expected to run into them so far north, but that's life. We picked up the arms in New Orleans and were intercepted just south of Belize. We doubled back and sheltered here. I have informers, too. So I know the damned Colombians are waiting for me down among the Half Moon Reefs. I'm still trying to figure out what to do about it."

He thought and said, "The Half Moons are unclaimed and off the big bulge in the coast where Honduras and Nicaragua meet, right?"

"Es verdad. They know we have to round that stretch of coast almost against the prevailing winds, depending mostly on our poor little engine to make any headway at all. It's a perfect ambush. I've been thinking about running north, where nobody's after me, and putting out to the high seas. We could probably make it sailing south along longitude eighty, well out to sea. But we're in a hurry. The shipment's already overdue, and our shore contacts in Panama can't risk waiting there forever."

He took a thoughtful drag on his cigar as he pulled her a bit closer and said, "Hmm. We seem to have diametrically opposite problems. Your enemies are waiting for *Nombre Nada* to the south, and our enemies are expecting *Flamenco Lass* to the north. Do you see what I see, doll face?"

Esperanza glanced down the length of their bodies and said. "No. You're still soft." Then she laughed and added, "Of course I see the opportunity for a ruse, Deek. But, tell me, is the *Flamenco Lass* as nice a vessel as my poor old *Nombre Nada?"*

"What can I tell you? The British schooner is new and well found. She has the latest in gear, new sails, a powerful auxiliary, and so forth. She's worth three times as much as *Nombre Nada* on the open market."

"Ah, but I am attached to my *Nombre Nada,* Deek."

"I know. So do half the customs officials on the Mosquito Coast. Folks in our line of work can't afford sentiment, Esperanza. We can't afford to repeat our patterns, either. The Colombians sitting on the Panamanian rebels have *Nombre Nada* on their shit list, and they probably have her outline posted on every gunboat they have looking for her."

Esperanza began to toy with his genitals as she said, "I told you I understood the picture, Deek. But I must have time to think."

So they dropped the subject as she raised another one. This time she got on top. It was a rather novel experience for Captain Gringo to play the passive partner, although he'd done so with Esperanza before, and most women got on top once or twice in the course of an orgy. Most women were not Esperanza. She didn't just fork her legs over his lap and make bouncy bouncy. She was powerfully built, and although her hips were broader than many a woman's, she used them like a man did when he made love. She lay full length atop him, legs together and down between his spread thighs, so that anyone looking in on them might have thought, for the moment, that a soft-looking boy was screwing the hell out of an amazingly muscular girl. Esperanza gripped his shaft inside her, almost painfully tightly in this position, and pounded her pubic bone against his as she kissed him passionately, obviously enjoying her mock dominance. She even ran her hands under his buttocks to lift his pelvis to meet her thrusts, as a man does to a woman whose derriere is too small. It felt weirdly good and he came fast as she almost milked it with her unusual motions. Then, not wanting her to think he was a sissy, Catpain Gringo growled in mock ferocity and rolled her over on her back, without withdrawing, Esperanza instantly went feminine and submissive, spreading her legs and arching her spine to take him in a manner that felt so different that it was like starting over again with a new partner. A very soft and yummy one. They climaxed together in moaning mutual pleasure.

Then, as he lay limp in her arms and love saddle, letting it soak inside her, Captain Gringo smiled down at her and said, "God damn, you're good, Esperanza!"

She smiled back and said, "You are not bad yourself. What do you suppose this magic is between us, Deek? We are not in love. People like us have no right to fall in love. But every time we get together, it feels so good I don't think it could be any better if we went crazy and got married."

He said, "I've missed you, too. Like I told you the last time, I think we enjoy each other so much because we're both knock-around bums who like and trust each other. Of course, you're not exactly deformed, either. I'd enjoy your body even if I hated you. But, yeah, it does get magic, doesn't it?"

She kissed him in an almost sisterly fashion, just to be affectionate, and said, "It feels nice to be in the arms of a real friend. It saves so much of the, how you say, bullsheet? I know I am very naughty. It is nice to know you know I am naughty and so it does not matter what I do or say. If I told you I wished for to be thrown to the floor and pissed on, you would not be shocked, eh?"

"Jesus, is that what you want to try next?"

"Of course not. I am not a freak. The point is that if I was, I think you would be a good sport about it. That is what I like about making love with you, Deek. You are as much a confidant as a lover."

He laughed and moved experimentally in her, but it wasn't ready yet, so he said, "Okay, confidentially, what do you say about the other deal? If we put out to sea separately, then met in a secluded cove to transfer gear and cargo, you could sail right past those gunboats by the Half Moons as the *Flamenco Lass,* a tub they don't have on their shit list. Meanwhile, me and mine could head north in the *Nombre Nada,* where everyone's out to stop the *Flamenco Lass,* see?"

She moved her hips as she sighed and said, "I said I was still thinking about it. Give me time, and give me some more loving. I have not had any for a long time. You know it is against my policy to have sex with any of my officers or crew."

"Yeah, the poor bastards. What do you do between ports, Esperanza?"

She giggled, hesitated, and said, "I masturbate. I could not tell that to any other man. But half the joy of being with you is that I can be myself completely. Do you ever masturbate, Deek?"

He felt his cheeks redden as he said, "Hell, nine out of ten people do, and the tenth one is a liar. But why are we talking about that now? I sure don't have to jerk off around *you!*"

She moved her hips faster and said, "I have a fantasy. I know you may think it is crazy, but . . ."

"Hey, if it doesn't hurt, I'm game."

She explained, "As you know, when one is lonely and, ah, trying to enjoy oneself, it is not enough to just think about plain sex. One must stimulate one's mind as well as one's own private parts to have a private orgasm, no?"

"Sure. We all make up sex adventures we'd never have the nerve to try in real life. There's nothing wrong with that. Incest and beastiality only count if you really commit them."

"It is odd we meet so soon after an idea I had the other night. You were in my dream, Deek."

"No shit? What crazy thing was I doing to you, honey?"

"Oh, you were behaving quite sedately. I was the perverse one. You see, when one is alone and desperate, one tends to use, ah, unusual tools in a quest for novelty."

"Yeah, you dames have a great advantage there. There's hardly anything a man can find that feels nearly as nice as a cunt. Gals get to use damned near anything tubular they can get inside them."

Esperanza laughed and said, "Let me up, and I'll show you something."

He rolled off her. She sat up, reached to the drawer of

69

her built-in bed table, and took out one of the damnedest dildos he'd ever seen.

It was an amazingly realistic pink rubber model of a male's running gear, balls and all, albeit at least a third larger than anyone was hung this side of a freak show. He marveled, "Jesus, can you really take all that, Esperanza? You're giving me an inferiority complex!"

She blushed as she said, "Do not worry. You are more than man enough for any woman, Deek. Actually, I *can't* take this toy all the way."

"Oh, but it's fun to try, right?"

"Yes. It is most stimulating. In the dark, alone, it feels most real, and it is indeed the best thing I've found for self-abuse, up to now."

He frowned down at the grotesque love toy in her hand and said, "Okay. You've shown me your secret lover. Where do I fit in to the picture?"

She couldn't look at him as she said, "I read about it in a dirty book, translated from the Arabic. Arabs are very imaginative. The other night as I was jerking off, as you call it, I remembered this story about an Arab girl with two lovers. One was making love to her from the front as the other entered her from, ah, behind."

He laughed and said, "I don't think it would work. Everybody's legs would get in the way."

She said, "True. But anyway, as I was stimulating myself, pretending this was someone nice, I got to wondering what it would feel like if someone else I liked was sodomizing me at the same time. Just thinking about it made me so excited I was nearly able to take this substitute almost to the roots."

"Naturally, in the front door?"

"Of course. I couldn't even get the head in the other way. I tried it once. Anyway, in my fantasy, you were making love to me from the rear, and now that you are here. . . ."

"I get the picture. Who was the other guy?"

"Nobody. When I am with you, I don't want anyone else intruding on these frank conversations. Some men are such bores in bed, the way they talk, talk, talk, saying things they do not mean and things they don't have to say."

He said, "Gotcha. Okay, I'm game. But I'm not sure this is supposed to work, Esperanza."

She laughed and rolled over on her hands and knees, presenting her big pale rump to him as she said, "First you put that other big thing in my pussy, eh?"

He grimaced but said, "That sounds like a good way to start," as he picked up the odd-feeling dildo. He got on his knees behind Esperanza and gingerly put the tip in place, muttering, "Open wide and say ah."

Esperanza said, "Oh, take it easy!" as he got the head in and slowly thrust the thick shaft into her vagina. He didn't see why it should be giving him an erection of his own, but it was. It felt dirty-innocent to watch what looked like another man's dong going into the pink paradise he'd just vacated. Esperanza took the dildo's base in her own hand, between her legs, and said, "Now, you mount me, naughty, as I move this the way I like it, no?"

That sounded reasonable. He rose, took a big, soft-skinned, muscular buttock in each hand, and spread them as he got his own, more normally proportioned tool in place between them. Thanks to the heat and earlier normal rutting, Esperanza's crotch needed no lubrication, although, in truth, he had a hell of a time getting the head in. After that, things went more smoothly. He knew he could hurt her if he wasn't careful, so he slid his shaft into her rectum gingerly. It felt tighter than it would have without the mass of India rubber stuffing her wider opening. It felt weird as hell when she moved the big dildo under his throbbing shaft. She moaned and said, "Oh, my God, I've never felt anything like this before, have you?"

"That's for sure! Can we do it the other way, now? This is hot as hell, but I'm afraid to let myself go this way, honey."

She arched her spine to take him deeper in her rectum as she hissed, "I want you to let yourself go! Treat me back there as you treat me up front! I assure you no part of me feels left out!"

So he shrugged and started throwing it to her dog style, moving faster and faster as he saw he wasn't hurting her. It wasn't hurting him, either. He felt himself starting to climax. He wanted to make it last. So he thrust deep and stopped, his full erection throbbing to the roots inside her pulsating rectum, while the crazy love toy, moving in and out on the other side of the partition of living flesh, literally jerked him off inside her.

He threw his head back, holding on to her rump with his hands as he fired a bigger load than he'd known he still had up into her bowels. He could tell by her contractions that she was coming, too. She suddenly sobbed and fell forward, off his shaft, leaving him kneeling there alone and somewhat left out as she finished herself with the dildo, taking it all the way in long savage thrusts.

As he lay down to recover, Esperanza rolled over, leaving the love toy in place, and crooned, "God, that was fantastico. I think I may have killed myself, though."

He laughed and said, "Yeah, I noticed. Was I as nice as your dream, honey?"

"Better. But I don't think we'd better ever do that again. My poor anus feels bruised, and I'm afraid to take this thing out. Where do you suppose all of it went? I didn't think I was that deep inside."

"Don't ask me. I was wondering, too."

Esperanza laughed and slowly withdrew the dildo, with a shudder and a sigh. As she put it aside, she giggled and said, *"Madre de Dios,* I'm still throbbing inside. I feel so empty, now. Ah, Deek?"

With a grin, he wiped himself off on the sheet and re-mounted her. As he entered her normally again, Esperanza sighed and said, "Oh, yes, this is ever so much friendlier. I think I'll stick to more sedate lovemaking from now on, but, Deek?"

"Yeah?"

"I don't want to be *too* sedate. Could you move a little faster?"

"Sure. But what about our other deal?"

"Just fuck me, you wonderful brute. You know you can have my damned boat. I want you to have *me* some more before we discuss things back on earth!"

The *Nombre Nada* left port on the evening tide, followed at a discreet interval by *Flamenco Lass.* In other parts of the world, telephones began to ring. The Columbian revenue service was informed that the gunrunning Esperanza and her cutthroat pro-rebel crew were sailing south as expected. Colombian naval units off the Half Moon Reefs would soon be notified by Marconi wireless to keep a sharp lookout for the familiar outlines of the *Nombre Nada.*

In Havana, an otherwise handsome military governor with cobra eyes learned that the *Flamenco Lass* had left Corozal. Butcher Weyler transferred the call to the head of Spanish Intelligence. What the British spy vessel had been up to in Corozal was still a mystery. But what did it matter, since everyone knew they were headed north?

The Spanish spy in Belize who'd tipped off his government had not been able to say just what the Brits were up to. But the details didn't matter to Butcher Weyler, who, despite his Dutch surname, had a Spanish hidalgo's abstract dislike for and distrust of the Anglo-Saxon breed. A man who herded Cuban cane cutters into concentration camps on mere suspicion saw no reason to take chances with any outsiders who might or might not be poking their noses into Spain's business. Whatever they were up to, he wanted *Flamenco Lass* blown out of the water.

When Sir Basil Hakim's phone rang, the Merchant of Death was enjoying an opium pipe at one end and a twelve-year-old virgin at the other. So he said merely to keep up the good work and relay the information to his agents up the coast. He knew what Greystoke was up to. He still hadn't figured out the best way to make money out of his inside information.

As the sun was setting, both schooners put into a deserted, mangrove-fringed cove that Esperanza knew about. The dead of *Flamenco Lass* had of course been buried at sea and the mess cleaned up by then. So the business at hand was the transfer of gear and cargo. It went smoothly. The few crew members on either schooner who'd grumbled had been dealt with earlier in the day back in Corozal. Rice's swollen jaw was feeling better, and Esperanza had graciously granted bed rest and a sling to the man whose arm she'd broken.

On deck, as they passed in the general bustle of both crews, Captain Gringo and Esperanza of course remained sedate and didn't even wink at each other. But when the last gear and cargo had been transferred and there was nothing more to keep the schooners moored side by side, Captain Gringo found Esperanza sitting rather wistfully on her new bunk in the repaired master stateroom of *Flamenco Lass*. He closed the door, sat beside her, and said, "I know," as he put an arm around her.

Esperanza said, "Jesus, Maria, y José, I wish we had time to say adios properly, Deek."

He nodded and cupped a big breast in his free hand as he replied, "I guess we could take time, if you're really hurting."

Esperanza laughed and said, "You know that there is no such think as a, how you say, quickie between you and me, *toro macho!* Just hold me for the moment before we part again."

So he did. Esperanza snuggled her head against his shoulder and said, "You know what I like about you best, old friend?"

"The fact that we are old friends, Esperanza?"

"Exactly! Any reasonably healthy man is fun to go to bed with. I think the magic I feel with you is that we like each other and can be frank and open. I can even tell you I do not wish for to fuck and you do not get hurt and angry like some others might."

He chuckled and replied, "As a matter of fact, I was wondering how I was going to get out of it, too. The stars are coming out and it won't stay dark forever."

"Ah, then you have had enough of me?"

"No man born of woman could ever get enough of you. But we'll meet again, if we manage to stay alive that long. One of the things I like best about you is that you're pragmatic about staying alive. I once had a dame with her dumb legs locked around me who wouldn't let go when I was trying to get at my gun in a hurry. But never mind, I shouldn't have said that. Sorry."

She laughed and said, "Don't ever be sorry with me, Deek. You know I have lost count of the men I've slept with, too. There is no need for jealousy between old comrades. By the way, have you fucked either of those English girls I noticed among your people? They are both very pretty. Which one is the best lay?"

He laughed, hugger her tighter, and said, "I don't know. So far I've only laid one of them."

"The blonde, right? A woman with strong feelings recognizes her sisters in sin. I wouldn't fool with the brunette if I were you. She strikes me as one of those complicated types."

He ran his hand down her bodice and into her lap as he said, "Neither one of them are my main mission. Listen, the door's locked, we're our own bosses now. So, what the hell?"

She shook her head and got to her feet, saying, "No. I want to, but not now. You are right about the starlight. I would rather gaze at the moon and stars in your arms tonight. But we don't have the time."

He nodded and rose to join her at the locked door. But as he started to slide the latch, Esperanza sighed, lifted her skirts, and leaned against the bulkhead, saying, "Do you promise only once?"

He took her in his arms, unbuttoned his fly, and they made love fully dressed and on their feet. It was not only a novel way to have Esperanza, but astonishingly stimulating. She was almost as tall as he was, so her bare legs were close together as he moved in and out of her pursed vaginal lips. She was able to move her pelvis to met his thrusts with gravity-free ease. They climaxed almost at once, together. Then, as he suggested another, she pleaded, "You promised!" and literally spit him out with her tight internal muscles. So, as she turned to let her skirt fall as she unlocked the door, he put his pecker back in his pants, buttoned them, and stepped out in the corridor. A crewman was passing, so, since she would be staying here, they shook hands gravely as she said, "Go with God, Deek, until we meet again!"

He nodded, turned, and went up on deck with a wistful expression on his face. He crossed the gangplank between the schooners, and when he boarded *Nombre Nada* he told the English bos'n, "That's all she wrote. Cast off all lines, weigh anchor, and let's get the hell out of here."

Gaston, Carmichael, and the helmsman asssigned to this watch were back in the cockpit, with one Maxim already set up. So, as his orders were carried out, Captain Gringo strode forward to see if the forward gun had been installed as ordered.

It had. As he lit a smoke, he saw by the match flare that Flora Manson was seated alone in the bows. He said, "Evening. We'll be putting out in a minute or two. What brings you up here? Don't you like your new stateroom?"

She said, "It's all right. I just like the air up here better. Do you suppose we could sleep up here, later tonight?"

"You can, if you like. This time I have my own quarters. Rank has its privileges, and we've been whittled down a bit. It's only fair to warn you that we make some green water over the bows, though. Now that I'm running things, we'll be standing farther out to sea. The swells will be steeper, but not as many people will be staring at our sails from shore, see?"

She sniffed and said, "I see very well indeed. I noticed you spent quite some time saying goodbye to that rather sluttish Spanish friend of yours."

He growled, "I agree Esperanza is a friend, so let's not call her a slut. This transfer may save all our lives!"

He took an angry puff on his cigar and added, "Let's get another thing straight, doll. I don't owe you any explanations about my relationships with other ladies, so let's knock off the cracks! We're not married, engaged, or even going steady. So I don't have to account to you whether I'm pure as the driven snow or the randy stud you seem to take me for!"

She smiled sarcastically and said, "I rather imagine the

latter description applies. Aside from what Phoebe told me, you were alone with that Esperanza longer than it usually takes to just say adios."

He laughed and said, "Thanks for the compliment. Since you seem to have been timing me, you must think I'm pretty fast on the draw!"

He had been rather fast, at that, but, noting the confused look on her face, he added, "You said you were married once. What were you married to, a jack rabbit?"

"I don't understand," she began. Then, since she did have a good watch, she blushed and added, "Oh."

"You've got to control your suspicious nature," he insisted. Enjoying his secret joke, he continued, "This may come as complete surprise to you, but I don't really spend every moment away from you fornicating. For a dame who worries so much about other people's morals, you sure seem to spend a lot of time thinking about the subject."

"You don't have to get nasty about it, Dick."

"I'm not the one that's being nasty. You are. Can't you get it through your pretty little head that what other people may or may not feel like doing is none of your fucking business?"

"Sir!" she gasped. "I'm not used to hearing language like that!"

"You'd better get used to it, then, if you're going to keep pestering people about their sex lives. Sure, you talk hoity-toity when you bring it up, but face it, doll—what you're really asking is whether I fucked Phoebe, or Esperanza, or both. And I'm telling you, less hoity-toity, that it's just none of your fucking business!"

She leaped to her feet and dashed out of sight, heading either for her stateroom or to leap overboard. He didn't really give a shit.

At least, he didn't think he gave a shit. But as he crouched behind the bow gun, checking the action, and the

Nombre Nada began to move, he was wistfully aware that Esperanza was leaving aboard another vessel and that good old Phoebe would probably be spending the night in Gaston's room. The bubbly blonde's anatomical problem gave Gaston's experienced tongue a distinct advantage between Phoebe's precocious thighs.

Nombre Nada's bluffer bows began to rise and fall under him as she headed out to sea, sails still furled and older but powerful steam screw churning. As ever on warm, dry nights along the Mosquito Coast, the waves were phosphorescent, and the blacked-out *Nombre Nada* seemed to be ghosting in a sea of cold green embers. The sky looked like purple velvet spangled with big tropic stars that looked close enough to shoot down. He grinned crookedly and muttered, "Smart move, Walker. You chased a dame away on a night few dames would stand a chance against!"

He tried to drop it. What was done was done, and it wouldn't kill him to behave himself for a while. But the damned luminous waves kept reminding him of that beautiful girl he'd met that time at a steamship rail, and heard her sweet, sad little poem about moonlit waves of fire. What had ever happened to her? Oh, yeah, she'd gotten killed. People did that a lot down here. He snapped the action closed on the Maxim and covered it with a tarp. His job wasn't laying dames. He had at least two on his hands he meant to bring back alive. This was no time to be mooning about less important pleasures.

But as he got to his feet and stared out across the water, looking for Esperanza's new vessel but unable to spot it against the ink-black lace of the mangroves, he muttered, "Dammit, Esperanza. If we'd torn off at least another one, I might not be in this fix right now!"

●　●　●

Captain Gringo's ruse was put to the test the next morning, when they encountered a Mexican gunboat steaming closer to the shore. The mate on the gunboat's bridge called his commander topside when the lookout spotted the British merchant ensign flying from *Nombre Nada*'s spanker.

The older and more relaxed Mexican skipper scanned the passing *Nombre Nada* through his binoculars for a moment before he lowered them and said, "I've seen that schooner before. She makes regular runs up and down this coast. She's not the one we've been told to watch for."

The mate said softly, "She flies the red ensign of los Anglos, my captain."

"What of it? We are in international waters and the British have a large merchant marine. Compose yourself, *muchacho*. Mexico has enough problems without picking fights with *los Anglos*. We only have orders to intercept that one British vessel. Let us not get ourselves excited every time we see the red ensign, eh?"

The mate glanced at a ship's silhouette thumbtacked to the rear bulkhead of the bridge as he said, "That schooner passing us at the moment does not seem to be wanted, I see now. Forgive me for being overzealous, my captain."

"Hey, *muchacho,* I told you to keep the eye peeled for British schooners. That particular one is not the one we were told about. But if it were, we'd both be in for decorations about now. *El Presidente* in the flesh has taken a personal interest in that British spy mission!"

The mate saw that the old man was in a good mood, so he asked, "May I ask why, my captain? That report says nothing about the British wishing to spy on Mexico."

The skipper shrugged and replied, "In God's truth, nobody knows who they mean to spy on. Our man in Belize was unable to find out. But he did find out that the notorious Captain Gringo and his comrade, Gaston Verrier, are both aboard *Flamenco Lass*. Whatever *los Anglos* are up to, those two madmen are wanted in Mexico for crimes too numerous to mention!"

"Yes, I have heard of this Captain Gringo. Our Mexican rebels seem to regard him as some sort of hero."

"*El Presidente* Diaz does not. The last time they passed through Mexico they almost wrecked the place. They are dangerous maniacs. They make our government very nervous, and Mexico City wants them out of business."

"I heard about the trains they wrecked in Mexico, my captain. Has anyone ever figured out why they behave so unpleasantly? Neither one can call himself a Mexican, rebel or not."

The skipper grimaced and said, "I understand they got into some sort of harmless brawl with *los rurales*. You know how some *rurales* are."

"Yes, they can act like maniacs, too."

"Agreed. But just because there was some little misunderstanding with our sometimes uncouth rural police, those two soldiers of fortune had no right to declare war on all Mexico!"

"What were *los rurales* doing to them when they went mad, my captain?"

"*Quien sabe?* Probably stealing their shoes or threatening to shoot them. Some of our *rurales* could use a bit more training. What *los rurales* did to them is not important. *Los rurales* have the right to do anything they like to almost anyone. The point is that this Captain Gringo took it out on all of Mexico. He joined up with Mexican rebels and machine-gunned innocent *federale* troops who were only trying to do their job. The man is a monster!"

"He sounds like one, my captain. May I ask what job *los federales* were trying to do when he murdered them?"

"Oh, they were trying to kill or capture Captain Gringo and his rebel friends. Perfectly legal. Captain Gringo simply does not understand or respect the laws of Mexico."

The skipper consulted the clock on the bulkhead and added, "Carry on, *muchacho*. I am going back to my quarters for now. I am engrossed in a good book, and I do not wish to be disturbed unless you really spot that Clyde-built schooner with the raked funnel and masts, eh?"

Aboard *Nombre Nada*, Captain Gringo was starting to breathe again as he crouched behind the tarp-covered, rear-mounted Maxim. Carmichael manned the helm as Gaston crouched beside Captain Gringo. Everyone else, of course, had been ordered to take cover. As the Mexican gunboat drew out of range, Captain Gringo chuckled and said, "It worked. I hope old Esperanza has the same luck with Colombian gunboats to the south!"

Gaston said, "We shall all need luck, if my old bones are not fibbing to me, *mon ami*. My bones are telling me to expect a visit from our old friend, the Carib god Hurikan."

Captain Gringo got up from behind the machine gun and sniffed the trade winds before lighting a cigar. The air smelled of sun and brine, and the winds blew dry for sea winds. There was no taste of brass in the air, and the overhead sky was a cloudless bowl of cobalt blue, not tinged with the puss green of heavy weather in the tropics. He lit his smoke and said, "Your bones are just hurting because you fuck too much for a man your age, Gaston. It's a beautiful day for sailing."

Gaston shrugged and said, "The hurricane season is always the best time of the year for sailing in these waters, between hurricanes."

Carmichael, at the wheel, cast a worried look at the horizon as he asked Captain Gringo, "Does he know something I don't, Walker? We do seem to be enjoying steady air in our canvas, and the ground swells are jolly smooth for this far off a lee coast."

Captain Gringo laughed and said, "You'll get used to

Gaston's bitching after you've known him awhile. He looks under the bed and checks the closet every night before he says his prayers."

Gaston looked hurt and said, "I never say prayers. I discovered long ago that if anyone is running this cruel world, he does not listen to complaints from his customers. As to my cautious habits, *merde alors,* how do you think I ever reached such an advanced age in such a surprising universe? I *have* found strangers under my bed and in many a closet in my time. And I still say I feel a heavy blow in my bones!"

Carmichael said, "I hope you're wrong. What's the form if we run into a full gale, chaps? I'm not familiar with these waters. Do we try for sea room or look for a sheltered cove?"

Captain Gringo said, "We head out to sea and then some. An unknown lee coast is dangerous even when it's friendly, and the Mosquito Coast ain't. Aside from zillions of uncharted reefs, shelter is widely spaced. You're ten times more likely to be blown into a mangrove swamp or a limestone cliff than you are a harbor."

Carmichael nodded and said, "Right. From the way her timbers groan, this old tub has weathered many a storm at sea. What's the form if we have to run the gale?"

"There isn't much form in a hurricane. The wind and waves just come at you any old way. Old Caribbean hands just batten down the hatches, take in every scrap of canvas, and hope they have enough ballast."

"What about sea anchors?"

"The Spanish galleys tried that in the old days and found it didn't work so hot. The wind may blow one way and the waves may be coming another. A powerless sailing craft just has to make like a cork and let the storm decide where it's going. If you're too close to shore or a reef, tough shit. If the storm lays you on your side, pray your ballast doesn't shift. Hurricanes are not nice people. But we do have the advantage of auxiliary power. So we can at least maintain enough headway with bare poles to steer into the worst waves. You know, of course, that nobody takes a real wave directly over the bow?"

"Coo, give me some credit for being a sailor, Walker. I get the picture, now. I don't like it much, but, as I said, she feels like a stout old tub, and I doubt she'll roll over if we can take most of the big ones on our port or starboard quarter."

The cabin hatch opened and Phoebe Chester stuck her blond head out to ask if she and the others could come out now. Captain Gringo glanced aft at the distant smoke plume of the Mexican gunboat and said, "Yeah. We seem to be in the clear at the moment."

The two girls came out, followed by some of the crewmen. The men sensed they might not belong around the binnacle with the big shots and drifted forward to enjoy the cooling wind across the deck as they waited for further orders. The two girls joined the three men around the wheel, of course. They hadn't been invited. But nobody minded. They added to the decor and were probably less likely to cause trouble there.

Flora Manson peered at the dark, fuzzy, distant shoreline to the west and asked where they were. Captain Gringo said, "Off Quintana Roo, Mexico. It's a territory, not a state. Not too many people live there."

Gaston snorted and chimed in, "The last time we were there, we ran into people enough. *Merde alors,* some of them were trying to kill us!"

Flora frowned and asked, "I thought Yucatán started just north of our British Honduras, Dick."

Captain Gringo explained, "Yes and no. According to Mexico, British Honduras is part of the Yucatán Peninsula, if we're talking about gross geography. The *estado* of Yucatán occupies only the north tip of the Yucatán Peninsula, see?"

"Oh. Are the natives civilized in Yucatán State?"

"Depends on what you call civilized, and whether they're for or against Mexico City. Don't worry about it. We're not going that far. The charts say the cable to Cuba parts company with the Mexican mainland near Cape Catoche, in uninhabited or officially uninhabited territory."

The diver, Carmichael, said, "I've been examining those charts. If we have it located right, the cable actually runs out to sea well south of the cape and threads through some islands called the Mujeres. What can you tell us about them?"

Captain Gringo asked, "Gaston?" and Gaston said, "*Las* Mujeres are *trés fatigue*. Yucatán seems to be a continuation of the same limestone formation that sits under Yankee Florida. So, everything is made out of chalky, *trés* ancient coral and sea shells, dry as the bone where the land is high and disgusting mud where it is not. The islands are little more than coral reefs thrust up from the sea bottom, for some odd reason. They are of little use to mankind. A few Indian and Mestizo squatters camp on the main Mujer, a disgusting place two or three miles across. There are two other Mujeres large enough to call islands. Nobody was living on them the last time I passed this way. The remaining Mujeres are just dots of limestone and coral sand scattered about to impede navigation."

Carmichael nodded and said, "The charts make sense, then. Obviously the continental shelf is shallower among those coral keys. How long do you expect us to take to get there, chaps?"

Captain Gringo said, "Twenty-four hours at the rate we're going."

"Coo, that means we'll be coming over a perishing strange horizon in the target area at sunrise! I've checked the bunker fuel Esperanza left aboard, and I must say she left her bunkers nearly full. We could get there before dawn if we asked the engine to add a few knots to our progress, what?"

Captain Gringo shook his head and said, "Steady as she goes. I had this same discussion with the late Boggs. The reason Esperanza left us with plenty of fuel is because she wasn't wasting any when the trades were fresh. This old tub wasn't built for speed, Carmichael. She's a native-built coastal trader. Her lines were designed by Caribbeans who knew their winds and water as well as their craft. Her hull was built to make her best headway heeled gently under sail. Esperanza had that boiler and engine added amidships as an afterthought, with emergencies in mind. At full throttle, *Nombre Nada*'s screw could only add about four knots to her speed under sail, and meanwhile, I checked those bunkers, too, and Esperanza loaded them with the cheapest crude she could get to burn at all. So, we'd be sending up enough smoke for a Mississippi steamboat long before we coaxed enough extra headway out of *Nombre Nada* to matter."

Gaston said, "I do not understand this sneaky business in any case, M'sieur Carmichael. Surely you intend to dive for the cable in broad day, *non?*"

Carmichael shook his head and said, "Not if I can bloody help it! Coo, we'd be taking bloody chances indeed if we were to dive by daylight. My plan was to drop over the side in the inky hours and splice into the ruddy cable under cover of darkness."

The two soldiers of fortune exchanged glances. Gaston said, *"Sacre bleu,* what is the point of all this skulking about in the dark? Do you enjoy being eaten by sharks?"

Captain Gringo said, "For once he's right. The best time to dive in shark-infested waters is high noon, when you can see them. They know you can see them, and what the hell, a man is bigger than most of the fish they eat. Most shark attacks in the Caribbean take place at dawn, dusk, or at night, in murky water. Sharks find their way in the dark like bats. So that's when they like to hunt."

Carmichael stuck out his chest for the girls and said, "I told you I've encountered shark in the Med. I'm not looking forward to meeting the bloody things. But if we were spotted diving in broad daylight by more dangerous enemies . . ."

Captain Gringo held up a hand to cut him off and said, "Hold it. You're not thinking. We're going to be in trouble if we're noticed by anyone near that cable crossing, day or night. How long do you reckon it will take you to go over the side, locate the cable, and tap it?"

"I'm not sure. It can't take me more than an hour. I can't stay down any longer unless I want to get the perishing bends. If the water is clear and shallow enough, my lads and I can probably locate the cable from the surface with our glass box. Once we have it spotted, it should take me, oh, half an hour to suit up, go down, and attach our tap."

Captain Gringo nodded and said, "Okay. We can see for miles in every direction, and anything important should be sending a smoke plume over the horizon. So, if a patrol craft comes along, we can haul you in long before it can get close enough to see what we're doing, right?"

"Coo, I never thought of that."

"He's ever so clever," said Phoebe Chester, tossing Captain Gringo a Mona Lisa smile. Jesus, had she worn Gaston out already?

Carmichael laughed ruefully and said, "You're right, now that I think about it. There seems to be more to this espionage business than one reads about in books."

"Real spies don't write many books. The first thing a knock-around guy learns is to never act sneaky when he doesn't have to. That's why Greystoke ordered us to fly the British merchant colors and why I've left them up there. A tyro would try to pass an English-speaking crew off as some local bunch with false colors. If anyone asks what we're doing off the Mujeres with diving gear, we're diving for sponge. How the hell were we to know there was a cable anywhere in the neighborhood, right?"

Flora Manson asked, "Are there any sponges where we're going, Dick?"

He looked blank. Gaston said, *"Mes non,* the current whipping around the corner of Yucatán discourages sedate sea growth. But, as Dick says, how are we crazy gringos to know this, *hein?"*

Captain Gringo was becoming bored by all the idle chatter, and he hadn't eaten breakfast yet. So he looked at his pocket watch and called out, "Okay, gang. It's about time to change the watch. You've played with the helm long enough, Carmichael. Take a couple of hours off."

He glanced forward, saw that the Welshman, Rice, was the closest crewman who knew how to man a helm, and called out, "Rice, relieve Lieutenant Carmichael at the helm."

Rice got to his feet and came aft, but he couldn't meet Captain Gringo's eyes as he grumbled, "I haven't had breakfast yet, look you."

Captain Gringo didn't feel like hitting him again, so he said, "I'll have them send you a sandwich from the galley. Take the wheel and hold her steady as she goes till somebody tells you different."

Rice didn't want to get hit again, either, so he did as he was told, and Carmichael moved toward the hatch, followed by Gaston, growling that he was *"trés affamé."* Captain Gringo was hungry, too. But he moved forward along the deck to see what the night sea air had done to the other machine gun in the bows.

The Maxim was okay. As he replaced the tarp over the heavily oiled metal, he heard feminine footsteps behind him and turned on his knee to smile up at Flora Manson and say, "We really have to stop meeting like this. My wife is becoming suspicious."

She didn't get it. She frowned and said, "Oh? I didn't know you were married."

He sighed and said, "Forget it. My mother told me never to play cards with strangers on a train or try to tell a Brit a joke. What can I do for you, Flora?"

"I'd like to change my quarters. I don't care where I'm quartered as long as it's not with that beastly little Phoebe Chester!"

He frowned and said, "Gee, we're running sort of low on rooms with a view. But what's the problem? I thought you and old Phoebe were on friendly terms, Flora."

The brunette sat on a hatch cover and gathered her skirt around her shins primly as she sniffed, "Not as friendly as Miss Chester seems to feel we ought to be."

He leaned on the rail across from her with a crooked quizzical smile and said, "I thought Gaston was, ah, taking care of her friendlier feelings, Flora."

Flora wrinkled her nose and sniffed, "Apparently not enough to satisfy her newest fad. You know I don't approve of the way you men have been carrying on with that silly blond tart, but frankly, I was relieved last night when she tiptoed out of our shared quarters to be with one or the other of you."

"Watch it, Flora."

"All right, I was glad she was slipping out to sneak into Gaston's cabin." She repressed a giggle as she added, "I peeked."

"I figured you had. But I'm missing something. How could old Phoebe possibly bother you if she was playing slap and tickle with somebody else in another room?"

"She came back to our quarters at dawn, of course. I gather, from the way she boasted, she'd had quite a night. But you see, she hadn't had enough. She suggested she and I . . . oh, I can't say it. It was all so beastly!"

"Oh boy! I've been worried about someone in the crew attacking one of you dames, I never expected you to attack each other!"

"Dammit, Dick, it's not funny! Wipe that silly grin off your face this instant!"

He didn't. He couldn't. But his voice was sympathetic as he said, "I can see you have a problem. What do you think we ought to do about it?"

"I was hoping you'd know. I've never dealt with a perishing lesbian before!"

He laughed and said, "They don't bother me much, either. Damned if I see why. Some of them are nice-looking, and it's not that I'm unwilling."

"Don't be beastly. I can't share quarters, even in day-time, with a madwoman who wants to commit crimes of nature with my body!"

He could think of some things he'd like to do with her body, too. Her tropic-weight white blouse and skirt hugged her curves nicely in the cool breeze across the deck. But he said soothingly, "Look, old Phoebe's just sort of, let's see, how can I put it?"

"Dirty?"

"That sounds fair. What I mean is that she's not vicious. She's just discovered, well, a new toy. So she's acting sort of silly. I don't think she'd try to force you to do anything you didn't want to do."

Flora shuddered and said, "I don't care. I'm afraid!" Then she buried her face in her hands and began to weep.

He moved over to sit beside her. He put a comforting arm around her waist. She flinched but didn't try to move away. So he said, "I'll talk to her. Or, better yet, I'll have Gaston talk to her. He has a way of explaining the facts of life to naughty children."

She kept her hands over her face as she sobbed, "I don't think anything will save me now. She's a monster!"

"Oh, for God's sake, Flora. She's a harmless, bubble-

90

headed sex maniac. You're a couple of inches taller than Phoebe, and, hmmm, I see you're both about the same weight, distributed different. You're built tougher and in a fight you could take her. But there's not going to be any fight, Flora. Phoebe's nuts, but she's not a real lesbian and she wouldn't know how to play butch and fem with you if she wanted to. You're making a mountain out of a molehill. Like I said, I'll have Gaston try to calm her down, and meanwhile you can just say no, can't you? You seem pretty good at fending off advances from everyone else."

"I do? In that case, sir, what is your perishing arm doing around my waist?"

"You want me to put it somewhere else?"

Before Flora could answer, the lookout Captain Gringo had sent up the main mast called out, "Sail ho! Off the starboard stern and closing fast!"

Captain Gringo let go of Flora and ran aft to join Rice in the cockpit. The Welshman had already moved inboard to keep the binnacle between him and the black dot overtaking them at astounding speed. Captain Gringo saw that the lookout had been wrong in calling "Sail ho!" That was the trouble with R.N. training. Nobody had taught him to yell "Speedboat ho!"

There was no sail. The craft didn't even have a mast, and the thin funnel rising amidships wasn't throwing enough smoke to see at this range. He knew it was powered by one of those new, internal-combustion engines. And it was powered good. The speedboat was about thirty feet long, painted a dull black, and moving with a real bone in its teeth as it parted the waves with its sharp prow. Despite its speed, it lay low in the water. The reason was obvious. There was one hell of a gang aboard her. They were crouched low for people enjoying a friendly social call, and he didn't think those were fishing poles they were holding!

Captain Gringo whipped the tarp off the stern machine gun as Rice pleaded, "Shoot them, look you! They're showing no colors, and I don't think they're looking for a friendly race, do you?"

"When you're right you're right, Rice. Hold her steady as she goes."

"When are you ever going to shoot that gun, Yank?"

"Let me worry about that. You just hold this fucking stern steady for me!"

Gaston came out, attracted by the commotion, took the situation in at a glance, and dropped beside Captain Gringo, saying, "Let me know when you need a fresh belt, Dick."

Captain Gringo said, "I can manage. Run up in the bows and get Flora Manson below, *muy pronto!*"

"Aha! And what have the two of you been doing up there, enjoying a sun bath?"

"God damn it, Gaston!"

"I am going. I am going. Does everyone have to be so surly just because more pirates are attacking?"

Captain Gringo didn't know if the speedboat closing fast was a pirate or a patrol boat. This far from shore, the point seemed academic. Whoever those other guys were, the two vessels had the sea to themselves. But he held his fire for the moment. There was an outside chance that they had some innocent reason for overtaking *Nombre Nada.* He'd given them a chance to hail him, if they wanted to.

They didn't. As the speedboat got within rifle range, someone aboard opened up on *Nombre Nada* with a machine gun and proceeded to chop hell out of her mahogany transom with hot lead!

Rice screamed in terror, abandoned the wheel, and dived for cover. So of course the schooner swung into the wind, broadside to the attacking speedboat, as Captain

Gringo called Rice's mother something awful and opened up with his own machine gun to return their fire.

The unexpected lurch of the schooner threw the enemy gunner off, and his next burst tap danced slugs along the fortunately cleared deck. Before he could lower his elevation and sweep the waterline, Captain Gringo opened up again and sent a stream of Maxim rounds through the speedboat's bow, raking her from stern to stern. Better yet, Gaston, up in the bows, opened up with the other machine gun aboard *Nombre Nada* at the same time. The results were dramatic. Gaston wasn't as good a machine gunner as Captain Gringo, but that didn't mean he was bad with a Maxim. The two soldiers of fortune traversed their separate streams of automatic fire like the blades of massive garden shears and pruned the speedboat and its crew like a hedge. Captain Gringo released his hot trigger and called out, "Hold your fire!" as he saw that the speedboat was dead in the water and sinking.

He looked over his shoulder to curse Rice back to the wheel. But he couldn't see him. One of Carmichael's other men came on deck, followed by Carmichael. So he snapped, "Somebody grab the fucking wheel!" and the burly Carmichael did so, calling back, "What's the course?"

"Tack about and let's see if any of those slobs are still afloat."

There was at least one survivor aboard the speedboat as it went under. They heard him scream, *"Ay, tiberones! por favor! Ayudeme en la nombre de Maria!"*

But by the time they got *Nombre Nada* back under control and tacked back to the floating wreckage, the sharks the poor bastard had been bitching about had reached him. As they hove to and scanned the oily water for signs of life, all they saw were some floating black planks and the fins of some late-arriving sharks, circling to see what all the fuss had been about. The ones who'd gotten there in time for breakfast were doubtless already on the bottom, picking their teeth.

Carmichael asked, "Coo, who were they?"

Captain Gringo said, "I don't know. They weren't on our side. They might have been the guys who smoked us up in Corozal. The sudden dash and machine-gun fire fit."

The girls and most of the others came up on deck and had to have the deal explained to them, too. It didn't make much sense the second time Captain Gringo heard it.

Phoebe Chester asked, "How could they have known we were aboard this new boat? Wasn't changing boats supposed to fool everybody?"

It was an amazingly good question when one considered who'd asked it. Captain Gringo said, "You can fool some of the people some of the time, like Abe said. That Mexican gunboat we passed a while back bought our ruse. Whoever these guys were, they didn't. Like Abe said, you can't fool all of the people all of the time."

Flora said, "I'll bet someone in Esperanza's crew betrayed us."

"Now that's a dumb idea from somebody I thought had more brains," he said. "Nobody gives away a plan when their life depends on it working, Flora. If anybody suspected we'd swapped vessels, those Colombian gunboats hunting Esperanza and company would be after the *Flamenco Lass,* not the *Nombre Nada.*"

Gaston ambled aft and, having overheard the last few words, chimed in, *"Merde alors,* it is all so obvious, *mes infants.* These mysterious attackers were the same ones who hit us in Corozal and deprived us of Captain Boggs's services. Their craft was black and low in the water, so it was invisible at night and, hugging the coast, invisible by day as well."

Captain Gringo nodded and said, "Gotcha. They shot

up *Flamenco Lass,* lay doggo, watching, as a nondescript bump on the water, then followed us when we left the harbor. Both schooners' sails were outlined for them against the night sky."

Carmichael asked, "In that case, why did they wait so long before their second attack?"

"Easy. They probably did intend to hit us just outside Corozal. Then they saw us join forces with Esperanza, and if they knew enough Spanish to worry about sharks in the lingo, they knew better than to mess with old Esperanza and her boys. They shadowed us, waiting for a chance, see?"

"You mean, into that hidden cove?"

"Hell, no—would you follow two armed vessels into a cove with the shoreline behind them and the open horizon at your back? They waited out whatever we were doing. Then when they spotted our sails putting out to sea again, they must have spent some time talking over their next move."

"Oh, right. We and the *Flamenco Lass* were both going the wrong way. Must have confused them a bit, what?"

"Yeah. They decided to follow us, in the end, because we were headed the way a British mission would. They probably lost some time shadowing Esperanza long enough to make sure she was really headed south. Anyway, they had to stay close to shore so we wouldn't see them. The surf is rougher, closer in. That cost them more time. Then they had to wait out that Mexican gunboat when they spotted its smoke as well as our sails to seaward."

Flora smiled and said, "Then they couldn't have been Mexicans!"

"Not Mexicans the Mexican navy might approve of. That still leaves a lot of people for them to have been working for. Damn, I wish we could have taken at least one of them alive. Where's that Goddamn Rice?"

One of the enlisted crewmen said, "I saw him headed for the hold, sir. Do you want me to fetch him for you?"

Captain Gringo started to say yes. Then he asked Carmichael, "Is Rice any good to you at all?"

Carmichael said, "He's my pump man. Why?"

Captain Gringo shrugged and said, "Skip it. If I can't kill him, I don't want to see him just now."

As the day wore on, the sun of course got higher, and even out on the water it got hot as hell. Despite Gaston's bones, the sky was a big cloudless bowl with a white-hot, baleful sun glaring down out of it. The trades stayed brisk and steady. But, despite all the miles of open sea they'd blown across, the trades were notoriously warm for sea winds. As the tar began to bubble from between the deck planks of *Nombre Nada,* Captain Gringo went to Esperanza's quarters, now his, to have a sensible *siesta.* Some of his British companions, being greenhorns, regarded *la siesta* as a "perishing native custom," and tried to cool off on deck in the fetid breeze. As an old tropic hand by now, Captain Gringo knew that the secret of survival under a tropic sun was shade.

He opened the windward port and that helped a little. But Esperanza's recent quarters were muggy and, worse yet, still haunted by the earthy aroma of Esperanza. He slid open the drawer to see if she'd taken along her love toy. She had. He was sorry he'd peeked. It was bad enough to spend the next few hours alone on a cot while waiting for the sun to sink past four. A guy could wind up jerking off, lying naked on sheets that still smelled of Esperanza's exciting musk!

He took off his duds anyway. After shade, that was the second secret of *la siesta.* It didn't matter if one slept or not. In the tropics, even priests and nuns stripped to the buff and flopped across the nearest bed, alone or otherwise. He didn't feel like sleeping. He had nothing to read.

He'd trained himself to worry about the future as it arose, since nothing in his line of work ever seemed to go according to plan in any damned case. They were headed the right way, and it was up to Carmichael to dive for the damned cable and up to Phoebe and Flora to listen in and record the messages. He just had to worry about keeping them all alive while they did so. Up to now, he'd done okay. So, what the hell. If the Mexicans were not maintaining a heavy guard on the cable, they'd get away with it. If Mexico had the cable guarded, they wouldn't. There was no way to guess at what they'd find when they reached the Mujeres, and they wouldn't be there for the rest of the day and the night. Nobody could plan the unplannable. The smart thing would be to catch some shut-eye. A knock-around guy never knew when he'd have a chance to take a nap or a piss. So he slept and pissed when he got a chance to, right?

Nothing happened. He didn't have to take a leak and he wasn't the least bit tired. But he forced himself to lie there naked on the bed, as the breeze through the port cooled his flesh at least a little.

There was a knock on the door. He muttered, "Shit," as he sat up and hauled on his pants. But he wasn't really sorry for any distraction as he went to unbolt the door. With any luck, it could be Phoebe.

It wasn't. It was Flora Manson. She was fully dressed, being a greenhorn. She looked dismayed at his naked chest and gasped, "You're not properly dressed!"

He frowned and asked, "Properly dressed for what? Are you coming in or going out, Flora?"

"I wanted to talk to you. But if you're in bed . . ."

"I'm not in bed, I'm standing here talking to you.

Meanwhile, the deck's rocking under us and I'm gonna sit down. You do whatever you want."

He moved back to his bunk and seated himself, automatically starting to reach for a smoke, then deciding not to. It was already pretty gamy in here.

Flora hesitated, then stepped inside. Either she or the sway of the schooner shut the door behind her. She asked, "Aren't there any chairs in here, Dick?"

He laughed and said, "Hey, if you find any, take them with you when you leave. It's sort of crowded in here."

She said, "So I notice," as she sniffed, then she perched on the end of the bunk, crossing her legs discreetly as she added, "Spanish people must have odd notions about perfume. Was this that Esperanza's room, Dick?"

"I guess it must have been. I never bought her any perfume. What's the story, Flora? You didn't come here to borrow a chair or perfume, did you?"

She lowered her eyes and said, "We were talking about my problem when that speedboat attacked us, remember?"

Actually, he'd forgotten about her troubles with Phoebe, if one wanted to call them troubles. But he said, "Oh, right. Phoebe keeps attacking you. This may not be delicate, but I've been wondering about that. Just what in hell do lesbians *do* to each other, Flora?"

"My God, how should I know? Do I look like a lesbian to you?"

"I'd have to study on that. Like I said, I've never been in bed with a real lesbian."

She jumped to her feet and ran over to stand with her back to the door and one hand on the latch as she gasped, "I wasn't in bed with you! I was only sitting down!"

He laughed, patted the mattress beside him, and said, "Sit down some more, then. Look, kid, I know what's eating you. So I'll tell you up front that I won't make a lesbian advance, okay?"

"What about . . . other advances?"

"Hey, if you don't want me to leap on your bones, I won't, okay?"

She laughed despite herself and said, "That's a very grotesque way to reassure a lady, Dick. Is that American slang for not getting cheeky with a lass?"

"Close enough. Look, if you're afraid I'll rape you, go someplace else. I'm getting a little tired of your insulting attitude."

"*I've* been insulting *you*? My God, how?"

"Your whole dumb attitude. Ever since we met, you've been assuming I'm lusting for your fair white body. Aren't you being a little arrogant, Flora? Who says I'm lusting for your fair white body at all? I wish dames like you would give a guy a little choice in the matter. You meet a guy and right away you think he's drooling over you, like you were the real bee's knees. It's always struck me as a bit presumptuous."

She moved back to the bunk and seated herself again as she sighed and said, "I stand corrected. I suppose next to the busty Phoebe and your fiery Esperanza, I must appear a mousy drab to you, eh, what?"

"Let's not get sickening about it. You're okay. Let's talk about old Phoebe. Are you sure this idea that she's lusting for you, too, isn't some more presumption on your part? I mean, even a lesbian has the right to pick and choose, right? What makes you so sure she's after you?"

"I told you, she told me. She came back from a self-confessed absolute orgy with that old Frenchman, and then she suggested we . . . oh, you know."

He could guess, knowing Phoebe's newfound enthusiasm for French lessons. But he shrugged and said, "We're just talking in circles, Flora. You're not in any real danger, and we don't have another cabin for you."

She said, "I was wondering if I could stay, well in here." Then, catching the glimmer of interest in his eye, she quickly added, "I meant we could trade places, of course!"

He frowned and said, "Not bloodly likely, as we Yanks put it. Why the hell would I want to trade cabins with you? Phoebe shares your cabin. Part time, at least."

She blushed and said, "I know. But I don't think you'd find her advances so distasteful, Dick."

Actually, it sounded like it might be interesting. But it was a little sticky and very presumptuous of Flora, so he shook his head and said, "No, thanks. I like these quarters just fine."

"But you could be with Phoebe half the time the other way, Dick."

"Big deal. I could be with her *here* if that was what I wanted. You're getting arrogant again. I told you last night, it's none of your business who I sleep with. Does Phoebe know you're trying to fix her up with me?"

"No, but why should she mind? Haven't you already had your way with her?"

He didn't answer. He thought he'd settled that point. Flora stared down at her hands as she twisted a kerchief in her lap and pleaded, "Please, Dick. I'm frightened. I want to sleep in here. I'd just die if I woke to find another woman . . . doing things to me."

He chuckled and said, "Yeah, I don't think I'd like to wake up in bed with a sissy, either."

"Have you ever had a homosexual experience, Dick?"

"No, have you?"

She didn't answer for a time, and her cheeks were scarlet when she nodded and said, "At school. One of the upper classmates. I had a schoolgirl crush on her; you know about those, of course?"

"I've had crushes on lots of schoolgirls. But you mean an innocent friendship, right?"

"Yes, it started out innocently. And then, one night when we were in bed together she . . . seduced me."

"Did it hurt?"

"Don't mock me, Dick. It took years for me to get over it. I don't think I did until I got married. I never allowed her to touch me again. I never even spoke to her again, but it . . . it felt wonderful."

He nodded sympathetically and said, "I can see how a thing like that could mess up a young virgin's mind. It would have been your first orgasm, right?"

A tear ran down her scarlet cheek as she looked away and said softly, "It disgusted me. It frightened me. But nothing I was ever to do to myself down there ever felt half so good, until I married."

He nodded and said, "I'm beginning to see the light. You're as much afraid of yourself as you are of silly little Phoebe, right?"

"I don't want to be a lesbian, Dick. Lesbians are sick and crazy. But after I refused her awful suggestions and left in a huff, I couldn't help remembering that first time, and . . . oh, Dick, I'm so scared. Let me stay in here tonight!"

"Okay. But that means with me, doll."

She blushed even redder and whispered, "Can I trust you?"

"Probably not. I'm a guy, not a saint or sissy."

She started to cry again. He moved closer to comfort her with an arm around her as he said soothingly, "Hey, we'll work something out." And he meant it. Now that he thought about it, he could see that moving Flora into Gaston's quarters, officially, would solve Flora's problem. It would doubtless raise eyebrows and maybe tempers among the others, but tough shit. If Phoebe didn't have to sneak back between her bed and Gaston's, Flora could just lock her damned door and forget about it.

He was about to offer this sensible way out, but Eros smiled on him, and before he could blow it with his big mouth, Flora nodded bravely and said, "So be it. If it's the only way to save myself from crimes against nature,

101

I'll just have to take the more honorable way out, as sinful as it may be in the eyes of the Church!"

He didn't know what in hell she was talking about until she started to unbutton her blouse. Even then, he couldn't believe it. He laughed incredulously and asked, "Are you saying you'd rather offer yourself to me than Phoebe?"

She said, "It's the lesser of two evils. But don't look so smug, you mean thing. You may have me at your mercy, but I assure you I have no intention of *enjoying* it!"

He took his arm back and thought about throwing her out. But there were footsteps in the corridor outside, and she had her blouse off now. Nasty as her mouth was, her breasts were perky little temptresses, and as she started to slide her skirt down over her slender hips, raising her firm derriere to do so, he saw she'd worn nothing under that, either. So, he shucked his own pants as he twisted on the bed to help her all the way out of the skirt, and Flora moved away to roll into a naked ball, hiding her face with her hands as she sobbed, "Please don't be vile."

He felt like saying something vile as he stretched out, naked, to take her in his arms. He tried to kiss her, but she hissed, "Just *do* it and get it over with, since I have no choice."

He thought, boy, your husband must have really enjoyed this ball breaking when he came home a little late. But he didn't say it aloud. He'd met ball breakers before, and, as the old Spanish proverb put it, "No real man can be castrated by a woman's lips."

As he gathered her in, in her infantile position she had her knees against his chest, presumably to protect her breasts from his vile embrace. That sounded fair. He ran his hand down her spine, enjoying the contrast between her body and his most recent lover. So far, she was smaller in every way than Esperanza, albeit almost as firm. She was much thinner and firmer, as well as darker, than the bubbly blond Phoebe. He got his palm against her tail bone and pulled her pelvis closer, with her folded legs pressed tight against his torso, knees on his chest and insteps in his hairy lap.

She felt what was rising between her toes, gasped, and moved her feet farther up his belly. It was still a long reach, but as his shaft twinged in place, its head parted the soft, moist gates of her paradise, and she gasped again.

As he tried, for chrissake, to get someplace, Flora resisted his deeper penetration with her folded legs and hissed, "You animal! Haven't you ever heard of fore-play?"

He laughed and asked, "What's the difference, as long as you're not going to enjoy it anyway?"

She called him a brute, sobbed, and went limp in his arms. He rolled her on her back and used his weight to thrust home. Despite her apparent attitude and the fact that she was more tightly built than anyone he'd met recently, he noticed she was well lubricated for such a frigid bitch. He noticed she was moving pretty good, too, below the waist. But when he tried to kiss her again she snapped, "Just satisfy yourself."

So he did. He forced her legs apart, hooked an elbow under each of Flora's knees, and proceeded to throw the blocks to her hard and deep. Her beautiful firm body was inspiring, her small perky breasts felt good against his naked chest, and she didn't seem to object to his kissing the side of her creamy neck as he creamed inside her. From the way she was contracting on his organ grinder, Captain Gringo suspected she was coming, too. So he kept going to be polite.

She said, "Surely not again? Haven't I satisfied you yet?"

He said, "No. But look, could I get you an aspirin or something if it feels so awful?"

She strangled a smile and said, "Oh, just go ahead and enjoy yourself. I'm resigned to the fact you're only interested in my body as a toy."

He said. "Not true. I have a mad desire to go down on your brain. Can we cut this bullshit and do this friendly, Flora? You know you like it."

"That's what all you men seem to think, isn't it?"

"Yeah, men are funny that way. A dame spends half her time making herself look sexy with powder and paint, bats her eyes at him, twitches her ass under his nose, and seems surprised when he takes her up on it. Of course men think flirty dames want it, Flora. How often have you seen a man make a pass at a *nun?*"

She laughed despite herself and absentmindedly locked her ankles over his naked, bouncing behind as she said, "It's still not fair. A girl can't help it if she's feminine and, well, desirable. Do you find me desirable, Dick?"

"Hell, no, I'm just doing this for practice. Do you want me to stop?"

"Do you want to?"

"No. I don't think I could. I was just being polite."

She laughed again and said, "That's very flattering, even though I know you don't mean it. Ah, could you move a little faster, as long as we have to do this?"

He grinned, withdrew, and rolled her onto her face to reenter her from the rear, with his legs folded under and her firm white buttocks against his lower belly. As she figured out what was going on back there, Flora raised her face from the sheets, arching her back nicely, and protested, "That's bestial, Dick! Nice people don't make love in this position!"

"Trust me, babe. You're not exactly a beast and I'm not very nice. You said you wanted it fast, right?"

She started to answer, then buried her face in the pillow and began to chew it as she moaned and raised her derriere higher to take his powerful thrusts deeper. She still refused to admit it when she came again. But he could tell. So he rolled her over again to finish right, himself, and this time as he came in Flora he let him kiss her. She kissed like a little girl, at first, keeping her lips pursed as his tongue quested and his hips kept moving. Then suddenly she was inhaling him at both ends and raking his sweaty back with her nails as she let go at last and really gave herself completely. When they came back to earth and found themselves cuddled and sharing a smoke on the moist sheets, Flora recovered enough to say, "Well, I hope the queen never hears about this, but I must say it seems less disgusting than giving myself to another woman."

"Gee, thanks. I'm sorry we don't have a Great Dane aboard. We might have worked out something even less unpleasant."

"Don't be nasty. Now that I've satisfied you, can I spend the rest of the voyage in this cabin?"

"Sure, but it's only fair to warn you I'm not completely satisfied yet."

She was relaxed enough to smile, Mona Lisa, as she murmured, "I suppose I'll just have to grit my teeth and think of the Empire. Ah, how often do you generally make love to your love slaves, Dick?"

"I can't say. I don't get many slaves, loving or otherwise. Most of the ladies I've made love to in my time have been volunteers."

"I'll bet you've made love to a lot of them, eh?"

"As many as I've been able to. You're not going to pull that virgin crap on me, are you, doll?"

"No, but I must say you have a romantic way with words. Do you talk to other women this way, Dick?"

"Not often. Most of the ladies I've been to bed with seemed to want to be romantic. I can talk romantic as hell to a real pal."

She sighed and said, "I've been trying to respond to you, Dick. I just don't know how."

"I noticed."

"You don't really want me to say things I don't feel, do you?"

"It might help. Look, kitten, you've been putting on an act you don't feel since the first time we locked eyes. I don't expect a lot of June Moon crap from anyone, but this schoolmarm-captured-by-barbarians act is just as phony, and a hell of a bore."

"What should I say to you, then?"

"What you feel like saying, of course. At the risk of shocking you, I'll tell you about a lady I had in this same bunk who was a lot more fun to be with."

She flinched away from him and gasped, "Esperanza! I *knew* you and she were more than friends!"

He pulled her back against him and said, "Wrong. We've never been more than friends. That's why we enjoy each other's bodies so much. I don't have to worry about speaking my mind to her, and she can say anything she likes to me. We've gone beyond teenage romance into a clean, healthy friendship between consenting adults."

"But you have made love to her?"

"I just said that. We tear off a piece every chance we get. Why go to strangers when you have a friend, see?"

She laughed a trifle wildly and said, "I could never be that open with a man."

He snuffed out their cigar, put his free hand in her lap, and parted her black bush with two fingers as he said, "I don't see why not, once you've been open here. You ought to try letting yourself go with your mind as well as your body sometime, Flora. It might be a novel thrill."

She closed her eyes and opened her thighs as she said,

"All right. I do like what you're doing to me down there. But I'm not in love with you. How's that?"

"It's the first honest thing you've said to me since we met. Did it hurt?"

She smiled dreamily and said, "No, it makes me feel more . . . relaxed. Can I say anything I like?"

"Those are the rules. I've been saying anything I felt like to you, haven't I?"

"You have indeed, and I confess, some of the things you say make me feel excited as well as indignant. What would you think if I told you I was excited by the way our bodies sweat when they're pressed together?"

"I'd say you were right. We humans waste a lot of soap and water trying to disguise the fact we're animals at heart. We're trained to think body odors and secretions are disgusting, but we're all really excited sexually by them."

"I can smell your maleness. Can you smell mine?"

"How could we miss, as stuffly as it is in here this afternoon? Take a deep breath and enjoy it, honey. Queen Vickie and Albert smelled like rutting beasts on their honeymoon or she wouldn't have had so many grandchildren."

Flora giggled, snuggling closer and placing a hand on the back of his to encourage its movements as she asked, "Do you think it's true what they said about Her Majesty and that Scottish butler, John Brown?"

"Why not, if they wanted to? Who did they hurt?"

"My perishing God! Do you think John Brown ever, ah, did it from the back like that to the *queen?*"

"He'd have looked pretty silly doing it to a king. Speaking of dog style, it's awfully warm in here and we haven't really done it right, yet."

"Are you suggesting we should, ah . . ."

"Fuck, baby. You might as well get used to the word if you're intending to spend the rest of this voyage with me. Yes, I'm going to fuck you again, because I can't come with my fingers and I feel you reaching for another come. Like I said, let's do it right."

She seemed far from unwilling, albeit confused, as he moved her into position on her hands and knees, with her upthrust derriere presented for him to take her standing upright with his knees against the edge of the bunk. As he took one small firm buttock in each hand and entered her once more, Flora gasped and said, "Oh, heavens, this reminds me of the way I saw a mare and a stallion do it when I was a little girl."

"Did you get a kick out of watching?"

She giggled and said, "I wondered what it felt like to them. Now I think I know. It feels ever so improper, but you're right about it being cooler and . . . Oh, yes, Dick! Fuck me this way! Fuck me hard and make me come like a horsey!"

So he did. Then he had her against the cabin bulkhead for a change of pace before they wound up back on the bed, with her on top, bouncing madly and laughing like a naughty child as she grinned down at him and repeated every forbidden word she'd ever heard. Some of them made little sense under the circumstances, since he was damned if he could see what they had to do with sex. But after she'd purged her Victorian mind of bile and come some more with her frustrated Victorian body, Flora was able to fall asleep in his arms with a contented, childish smile on her Mona Lisa lips.

The *siesta* wasn't over, so he managed to catch a few winks, too, before they woke up, laughing, and tore off another good clean piece.

As Captain Gringo had foreseen, *Nombre Nada* spotted the low Mujeres to the north early the next morning. The lookout aloft spotted no other sails or smoke plumes on the surrounding horizon. So, with Carmichael conning with his chart, they steamed into position between the two small coral keys where the underseas cable was said to run. They dropped anchor in mid-channel. As Carmichael and his divers' crew took the longboat to do some exploring, Captain Gringo left Gaston in command and took four common seamen and one Maxim with him to scout the nearby keys. The chart said they were deserted. They looked deserted. But as Robinson Crusoe could tell you, a guy just never knew.

The key to the north was. There was little more than some sea grape, palmetto, Spanish bayonet, and an old beer bottle on the little cow pat of crunchy white sand and rock.

But when they rowed over to the larger key to the south, Captain Gringo, in the gig's bow, spotted movement in the heavier brush. He armed the Maxim, told his crew to get ready to duck, and had them ground the bow on the gritty white beach.

He called out, "I see you there! We're honest men. If you're honest men, come and let's talk. I'm not going to say it again!"

There was a silence you could cut with a knife as the people in the bushes thought about that. But everybody knew what a machine gun was by now. So, a million years later, a thin old man in the straw hat and white pajamas of a Mexican peon came out of the greenery holding a white flour sack in one hand. As he waved the improvised truce flag, Captain Gringo let go of his machine gun and leaped ashore. He still had his .38 if the fully exposed and unarmed *pobrecito* went nuts.

He walked toward the brown old man, smiling, and said, "I am called Ricardo. We have come here to hunt for sponge, see?"

"*Mi casa es su casa,* Señor Ricardo. You will find no sponge in these waters. Some oysters and coral, perhaps.

And turtles. Many turtles. My people and me are camped here to hunt turtles to make soup for rich Americanos. I am called Miguelito and all of us are Cristianos. Are you going to arrest us?"

Captain Gringo shook his head. If old Miguelito didn't know the British merchant ensign from the flag of Mexico, there was really no reason to educate him. Captain Gringo said, "No. It is not unlawful to hunt turtles. I just want to look around."

Miguelito nodded and said, "As I said, señor, *mi casa es su casa*. Follow me, *por favor*."

Captain Gringo told his boat crew to watch the gig, then followed Miguelito as he bulled through a wall of sea grape. On the far side, thanks to the shade of a palmetto, the chalky soil was weed-free. The natives had set up a primitive camp, with palmetto-thatched lean-tos around an open work space. The air was filled with flies and the God-awful stench of rancid turtle fat. A pile of big sea-turtle shells rotted, covered with flies, near a cannibal pot over a camp fire. The American visitor tried to ignore the disgusting conditions of the camp as he looked over its inhabitants. There were about a dozen men and four women. Only one of the women, actually a girl of about sixteen, escaped being ugly, and the young *muchacha* didn't do a hell of a lot for him.

Her figure was nice under her thin white cotton smock of flour sacking. Her face was okay but was smeared with wood ash and grease. She could have used a shampoo as well as a bath. Her long black hair looked like nesting bats had been eating in bed. Miguelito told him her name was Veronica. He hadn't asked, but he nodded at her anyway, and she looked away sullenly.

By the time he'd been introduced all around and invited to share some home-brewed pulque, Captain Gringo was really more interested in breathing air again. But he'd been raised politely and he knew the form. So, he sat on a log and let Veronica feed him a cup of dreadful pulque. He'd never really learned to like it when it came in a bottle. In a tin cup, with a fly doing the backstroke in it, he had to make a real effort. But he swallowed enough to be polite as he casually asked his hosts if they'd noticed any other "sportsmen" in the area.

Miguelito said, "Hardly anyone ever comes out to these keys, señor. That is why there are so many turtles."

He turned to a big burly Mexican with a badly scarred face and asked, "Have you seen any sponge on the bottom around here, Alejandro?"

Alejandro shook his head and said, "Not enough to bother with. Some few, in the lee of coral heads, where they can seek shelter against the current. Only hard things grow in these waters."

Captain Gringo thought the scars looked like they'd been made by shark teeth. He nodded pleasantly at Alejandro and asked, "Are you a diver, señor?"

Alejandro shook his head and said, "No. It was a woman with a broken bottle and an evil disposition. But you can see the bottom out there as you search for turtles on a clear day. The water is not deep."

Captain Gringo had noticed that when they'd anchored in perhaps forty feet of water, mid-channel. He asked, "Do you catch the turtles on the surface, then?"

Alejandro laughed and said, "We don't catch them anywhere. We harpoon them. During the mating season they come up on the playas to lay eggs and make love. The rest of the time one must hunt them at sea. They spend most of their lives in the water."

Another Mexican, with a drunkard's leer, said, "They even fuck in the water. I have seen them. Did you know a turtle has a cock much like a man's?"

Captain Gringo didn't answer, and he didn't look at

111

any of the women. He finished his drink, spit out the fly, and said, "I must be getting back to my schooner. Is there anything we can do for you people, as long as we seem to be neighbors?"

The Mexicans looked surprised. Alejandro asked, "Why and how can you help us, señor? Do you have turtles?"

"No, but we could spare some matches, coffee, things like that."

"Do you take us for begging *pobrecito Indios?* By the beard of Christ, we came out here to kill turtles, not to seek charity!"

Old Miguelito said, *"Silencio,* Alejandro! Can you not see the señor is trying to be *simpático?"* He turned to the American and said, "We, too, wish to be good neighbors, señor. But, I assure you, we need nothing."

Captain Gringo nodded and got to his feet, and the old man escorted him back to the beach. They shook hands, and Captain Gringo went back to *Nombre Nada* in the gig.

He joined Gaston on deck just as Carmichael and his crew were returning from their surface scout. Carmichael held up his black-lined wooden box with the glass pane in one end and said, "Duck soup! The cable is running in plain sight across the coral flats, and we can splice into it anywhere. I'll just slip into my diving outfit, and my part of the mission will be over before noon!"

Carmichael and his helpers went below to haul out the stuff they'd need, as Captain Gringo filled Gaston in on the Mexican turtle hunters. Gaston nodded and said, *"Eh bien,* if the Mexican navy took a serious interest in this area, you would not find peon poachers here."

"Poachers, Gaston? I didn't think turtle hunting was illegal."

"It's not, if you cross the gypsy's palm with silver.

Diaz has a tax on turtles, sponge, pearls, or anything that can be easily taxed. Did they show you a *federale* fishing license? Of course not. As I said, it's a good sign. It means these keys are not patrolled often."

Carmichael and his men dragged the diving gear out on deck. Others, including the two girls, naturally came out to watch as they made the Scot ready to walk the bottom. Captain Gringo had been down in a hard hat a couple of times. The last time had almost killed him. So, he was able to follow their moves as they got Carmichael suited up and screwed the brass helmet in place. His crew was good. Even the surly Rice seemed to know what he was doing as he set up the boxy air compressor and checked the valves. The compressor was run by hand. A wheel the size of a bike wheel, albeit cast iron and heavier, had to be spun by hand to work the simple air pumps, two of them, inside the box. Naturally, the rubber hose air line ran from the top of Carmichael's helmet to the pumps. Right now he had the air line coiled over one canvas-covered arm like a cowhand's throw rope, so he could pay it out as he moved across the bottom. The lifeline, simply a stout manila rope like a cowhand really would use, worked the other way. It was attached to the harness of Carmichael's suit, but the coils lay on the deck. His helpers topside would pay it out to him as he moved on the bottom, signaling with jerks when he wanted more or, if he jerked hard thrice, wanted to be hauled in pronto.

The diver's boots were lead soled. He had other lead weights in the canvas pockets of his web belt. Once filled with air, the suit would float if it wasn't ballasted.

Carmichael got unsteadily to his feet in the clumsy suit, closed the glass port of his helmet, and signaled Rice, who started pumping at once. The suit ballooned, making the diver look even more clumsy. Two men helped him to the ladder running down *Nombre Nada*'s side. Carmichael waved and proceeded down it with no further ceremony, as bubbly Phoebe called out to be careful.

Gaston didn't call out. He knew that with the vent of his helmet hissing like that, Carmichael couldn't hear too well. But he looked around as he muttered, *"Sacre,* everyone is in such a hurry! I would have made sure there were no sharks before I skipped so lightly overboard!"

Captain Gringo frowned but didn't say anything. He hadn't spotted any fins cruising the channel on his own scouting expedition, and obviously Carmichael and his men hadn't. The guy had a knife strapped to one leg and a whole tool kit strapped to his chest.

As he got waist deep in the calm water, one of the British technicians handed down the end of the thick insulated wire Carmichael was supposed to tap the cable with. Carmichael wrapped a couple of turns of it around his free arm and vanished below the surface for a moment. But then, as they leaned over, they could see his bubble plume and even see Carmichael as he dropped slowly to the white bottom. He landed in a cloud of coral silt, got his bearings, and slowly plodded out of sight, as Captain Gringo turned to one of the men paying out his lifeline to ask how far the cable was. The man said it was less than a quarter mile. Captain Gringo wondered why Carmichael had chosen to do it the hard way. If it had been he down there, Captain Gringo would have moved *Nombre Nada* right over the damned cable.

He lit a smoke and put a foot up on the bulwarks as he watched the bubbles breaking the surface farther and farther away. Flora joined him. She whispered, "Dick, do you think anyone knows?"

He frowned down at her and said, "About what? Us? I haven't been bragging in the forecastle. Have you?"

"No, but I've gotten some odd looks."

"Don't look odd, then. Pretty dames always get looked

at. Can we save that for later, honey? I'm kind of busy right now."

She whispered, "You know what I'm saving for you, you brute. I can hardly wait for the sun to go down again."

"Right. Meanwhile, it's up, and I'm watching for fins." He looked up and called, "Lookout! Can you see Lieutenant Carmichael from up there?"

No answer. He frowned and asked Gaston, "Hey, Gaston, who the hell's supposed to be up in the shrouds right now?"

Gaston looked blank. Captain Gringo cursed and said, "Right, ask a stupid question and you get a stupid old man staring back at you!" He turned, spotted a sailor who didn't seem to be doing anything important, and snapped, "You, Collins, up the main mast, and yell a lot if you see anything but the lieutenant on the bottom!"

Collins aye-ayed him and started up the shrouds. But before he got to the top, other things started to go wrong.

The Welshman, Rice, yelled, "Haul him in, look you! The pressure's gone, you see!"

Rice spun his pump wheel harder, face ashen, as, out on the water, Carmichael's severed hose popped to the surface and lashed around like a headless snake hissing air from its still-living lungs!

The linemen started hauling in hand over hand as, out on the water, a dark triangle broke the surface, moved a few paces slowly, then sank out of sight again. Captain Gringo whipped out his .38 and fired, of course, but even if the sonofabitch had stayed on the surface it was just out of range. The revolver slug splashed uselessly, well short.

Captain Gringo moved to help the linemen. But he saw that he'd only be in the way. They knew what they were doing, and they were doing it as fast as was humanly possible. It still took forever before they saw Carmichael's limp form at the end of the line below. Captain Gringo grabbed a length of line, hooped it over his shoulder, and plowed across the deck with it to help haul the dead weight out of the water.

It was literally dead weight. As they stretched Carmichael's limp form on the deck and removed his brass helmet, the water inside ran out over his calm, waxy features. It helped wash the vomit away. But it didn't help Carmichael. He had drowned.

By this time, Rice had stopped pumping and had hauled in the severed air line. As Captain Gringo joined him, the Welshman held up the end and said, "Bitten through clean as a whistle, look you! The creature must have had teeth like shears!"

Captain Gringo nodded and said, "Yeah. Are any of you other guys divers?"

Rice looked even more upset and replied, "Divers? Of course none of us are divers! Lieutenant Carmichael was the diver, you see!"

Gaston joined them, saying, *"Eh bien,* it is over. Without a tap attached to that mysterious cable, all we can accomplish by staying here now is to offer ourselves for target practice. I would say the mission is over, Dick. Would not you?"

Captain Gringo shook his head and said, "No. I'm not the diver Carmichael was. But I have been down. Rice, we seem to have recovered everything in good enough shape to fix. I'm still going to need your help, though. This isn't the gear I'm used to. So you and the others are going to have to show me the ropes."

Rice looked surprised. Captain Gringo nodded and said, "Yeah, I don't like you much, either. Are you willing to shake and forget it?"

The Welshman held out his hand uncertainly and said, "I'm surprised you feel you can trust me, Yank."

"So am I. That's the most complicated thing about my business. I wind up having to trust the damnedest people.

Come on, Gaston. We have to get this show on the road."

As they moved to rejoin the group around the dead diver, Flora was holding Carmichael's head in her lap, as if that were going to do him a bit of good. Blond Phoebe asked, "Are we going to bury him at sea, like the others, Dick?"

He shook his head and said, "Not for now. Not until we reach deeper water and away from the friendly neighborhood sharks."

Gaston said, "This idiot is going to try and take Carmichael's place. Can't one of you help me talk him out of it?"

Both girls started to, of course, and some of the men in the crew seemed to think he was nuts. One of the linemen said, "The lieutenant was one of the best. If he couldn't do it, you can't do it, Yank!"

Captain Gringo said, "Yeah. Get him out of that suit, dry it out, and splice the air hose. Better yet, since it was severed close to the helmet, just trim the end and reattach it. That ought to hold."

"Do you have any notion of the risk you'll be taking, Yank?"

"Probably not. That's why I intend to take it. Let's get cracking."

Captain Gringo planned his dive for that afternoon, in the heat of the day. For one thing, the suit would be dry, the light on the bottom would be better, and the sharks would be as calmed down as they ever got around here. For another, he needed time to study the problem. There was no sense in leaping overboard and hoping for the best unless he had some idea what the hell he was supposed to do down there.

His first move was to study the charts and move

Nombre Nada right over the cable. That didn't take long. But as he really studied the situation for the first time, he wasn't sure it made sense, either. He told the British bos'n, Clarke, "I'd have strung that cable farther north if I'd been asked to do it."

Clarke shrugged and said, "I would have too, sir. But they didn't ask you or me. British Intelligence told us it would be here. We found it here. So, why worry about what the Spanish or Mexican cable crews had in mind when they laid it on the sea bed?"

"I worry a lot about the Mexicans and Spanish, Clarke. They keep trying to kill me. Okay, we have the cable under our keel. We'll find out why once we listen in."

He took Flora and her tapping crew aside and asked to be filled in more on just how one tapped an undersea cable. A vapid young man who looked almost as feminine as Flora explained that you didn't actually cut in to the main cable. He said, "You wrap the end of our tap around it to form an induction coil. Eddy currents enable us to listen in without damaging or leaving a trace on the main cable, see?"

"Gotcha. I took general science in high school. Okay, if I just have to coil wire around the cable, it ought to come free with a good stout jerk if we have to leave in a hurry, right?"

"Of course. That's part of the beauty of an induction coil. All the really sophisticated equipment stays up here, in this salon."

Flora opened what looked like a suitcase and said, "I'll show you how some of it works, Dick. Do you know what this is?"

"Sure, a gramophone. I didn't know we had a record player aboard, Flora."

"It's not a regular gramophone. It records the signal the tap picks up. We can leave it on even when we have to leave the room. Better yet, we can slow the record down so that Phoebe can transcribe it to shorthand easily. If she misses anything, she can play it over."

"Neat. What exactly do you do, Flora?"

She blushed and looked away as she said, "I'm the cryptographer on the team. I search for codes hidden in the messages, and . . ."

"Gotcha. I mostly wanted to know how to tap the line, and you kids have told me all I need to know about my end of the wire."

He headed for his own quarters, stopping along the way to pick up some items from the ship's stores. So, he was seated on the bunk, lashing a butcher knife from the galley to a swab handle with wire, when Flora joined him there. She closed the door behind her, He said; "Leave it open. I've been getting a little breeze through the port with the door ajar, but it's still hot as hell in here."

She did as he asked, with a hurt look, and came to sit beside him as she asked what he was making. He said, "Shark spear, I hope. That diver's knife attached to the suit is pretty iffy, when you think about it. By the time a shark gets close enough to stab with a knife in your *hand*, he could have said hand in his mouth to the elbow!"

She said, "Brrr! I wish there was some other way to tap the cable."

"So do I. But there isn't. Look at the bright side. I'll be dropping straight down on it, at the safest time of the day. So, with luck, we'll know in just a little while if Greystoke's hunch about that cable was right or not."

She looked puzzled, so he explained, "He was too cute to tell us. But I figured it out. He doesn't expect us to tap a regular cable. For one thing, you and Phoebe would be drowned in noise. How in hell could you girls keep tabs on all the communications zipping back and forth along a public line?"

"We've been worried about that. Even with the gramophone recording every message, a lot of messages are sent in a day."

"Hell, a lot of messages are sent in an hour! You'd be listening in on everything from stock market quotations to lovers' spats, and Cubans talk faster than most other Spanish speakers. Greystoke suspects this particular cable is military. A private line."

"Oh? How do you know, Dick?"

"I don't know. Neither does Greystoke. That's why he sent us. The cable is new. It would be crudded up with sea growth if it had been on the bottom long enough to matter. It's laid inconveniently south, in waters hardly anyone ever visits. So our real mission is to find out who laid it. Butcher Weyler and *el Presidente* Diaz may have a private understanding neither Washington nor London knows about, see?"

Flora frowned and said, "No, I don't see. Diaz is supposed to be allied with the U.S. They say he's part Indian, and wasn't that the whole point of Mexico's revolt from Spain? Mestizos and pure Spanish Gachupines don't *like* each other, Dick."

"What can I tell you? Diaz doesn't like anybody, least of all gringos. But he knows where his bread is buttered. He'll also do anything for a fast peso. He could doublecross the U.S. on Cuba if Spain made him a better offer. On the other hand, for all we know, that cable was laid by Cuban rebels, and they could be plotting with damned near anybody on the mainland. This neck of the ocean was made for running guns. But look, why speculate? Let's tap the damned line and find out!"

She put a hand on his knee and asked, "Do you have to dive right now?"

He laughed and said, "Cut it out, you're giving me a hard-on. You know I'd rather wrestle with you than a shark, babe. But I have to save my strength." He consulted his watch and added, "It's almost time. I have to go on deck in a few minutes, so behave yourself."

She said, "Hurry back, then. I confess you've awakened some feelings I never knew I had. It felt so good last night, to let myself go completely in a man's arms. I don't mean just the lovemaking. I mean the way we talked about it so openly. I'd never done that before, even with my late husband. Do other girls like to let their hair down like that, Dick?"

"Everybody does. But we're raised so prudishly that half the married people in the world have never seen each other naked in broad day. A lot of couples would be happier if they could only get over the notion that you have to be ladies and gents, even when you're screwing."

"I've gotten used to calling it fucking, and I like it. I've been thinking about some things we haven't tried yet, Dick. Things I've always wondered about. Now that I can speak so freely . . ."

"Later," he cut in with a chuckle, adding, "I'm sure going to look silly in that diving suit with a hard-on." Then, since he had as curious a nature as most men, he asked, "What did you have in mind, in case I get back with all my important parts still attached?"

She blushed slightly and murmured, "Well, I've been talking to Phoebe."

"Yeah? I thought you were afraid of her seducing you, doll."

"I used to be. I'm not worried about having to resist temptation now. To be frank, I was tired of her bragging, and, well, maybe I bragged a bit, too. It seems I'm a couple of positions up on her, you horrid thing."

He laughed and answered, "What can I tell you? We didn't have as much time. Get to the point, I gotta go."

"Well, have you ever taken part in an orgy, Dick?"

"Not recently," he lied. "Why?"

"Phoebe says she has, and it's fun. So we were wondering if later this evening . . ."

"You're kidding! You, me, Phoebe, and Gaston all in a row? It sounds a little sticky, doll. Since we're playing True Confessions, I have shared a dame with another guy in my time. But it makes me nervous."

She said, "Silly, we didn't intend to invite Gaston along. Phoebe says she'll satisfy him and then join us here later.

"Phoebe would. But what the hell will you get out of the deal, doll? Don't you want me to give you my undivided attention tonight?"

She grinned like a naughty child and explained, "Phoebe says it's a good way to get over unreasonable jealousy. I told her we were, ah, just comrades in *amours,* but I confessed I was still a little miffed about you and her. Phoebe says that if I actually watched you make love to another girl while you, ah, played with me or something . . ."

"Gotcha. We'll work something out later. Speaking about people with odd sexual views, I've been wondering about that electrician working the eavesdropping gear with you girls."

"Which one, Clarke or Chadwick? They're both pansies."

"Oh? I figured little Chadwick walked sort of funny. Didn't take Clarke for a mariposa, though. How do you girls know?"

"Phoebe found out. When neither of them made a pass at her back in Belize, she peeked. She says Clarke is the boy and Chadwick is the girl. Why do you ask? Surely you don't want to try that, do you?"

"I'm saving that for my old age, after I've made love to all the women in the world. Okay, I guess we don't have to worry about your coworkers getting jealous if you spend too much time in bed with the boss. Get your hand off my fly, and let's see what's going on down there on the sea bottom."

Captain Gringo knew he'd made a mistake as soon as they closed the faceplate of the helmet. The rubberized canvas will still damp and sticky, and the helmet had been left out in the hot sun too long and smelled like the inside of a brass cannon that had been fired recently. Rice had shown him how to adjust the helmet valve. But there was no need to as he went down the ladder into the water, dragging air line, lifeline, and tap line after him as he tried to hang on to his improvised spear. The air hissed out the relief valve, but there was little sound from the intake over his scalp, since the suit was already pressurized. As he dropped completely below the surface, his ears were filled with the sound of his rising bubbles. He started to feel cooler at once, of course, but the inside of the suit still smelled like old gym socks and brass polish. He got to the bottom of the ladder and let go. His suit weights pulled him slowly to the bottom. Too slowly. He reached up and let some air out to drop faster. He knew sharks were more likely to attack near the surface.

Yeah, there were sharks. Hammerheads. The lookout had spotted them before he'd gone over the side. Some idiot had suggested shooting at them, but Gaston had told him he was an idiot, so there was no shark blood in the water to upset the balance of nature.

As his weighted feet hit bottom and he was enveloped knee deep in milky silt, Captain Gringo saw that nature was still balanced. He could see clearly about fifty yards in all directions if he moved his head and shoulders together in the clumsy rig. He was in the shadow of the schooner's hull and hence appeared as a mysterious, bubble-breathing black something to the hammerheads as they circled in the distance like Indians around a wagon camp. He hoped they were just curious. Hammerheads were ugly sonsofbitches as they moved their weird heads from side to side, sniffing. But hammerheads played to mixed reviews and weren't considered maneaters, most of the time. Gaston said that native pearl divers were less afraid of hammerheads than of tigers or lemons. But every once in a while someone caught a hammerhead with a human arm or leg in its belly, so it wasn't a good idea to pet one. They were most likely to attack in poor visibility or at any time if they smelled blood in the water. So, Captain Gringo reminded himself to be careful about skinning any knuckles as he plodded over to the nearby cable, dropped in slow motion to his knees, and stood the spear on end in the sand. The hammerheads just kept circling. So, he moved with slow, deliberate motions as he picked up a length of the heavy cable and wedged a loose block of dead coral under it. Even so, the slight disturbance of the silty bottom clouded the water around him as if someone had spilled milk in it.

But the charts were right about the current. It wasn't as strong here in the channel between two keys, but the silt cloud drifted away like cigar smoke in a gentle draft. He started wrapping the induction coil around the cable, keeping the turns neat and even as the rather fussy Clarke had warned him he must. Captain Gringo knew enough about electricity to understand why. The eddy currents running through the insulated cable would be garbled if the coil picking them up was sloppy. Hence, the job took much longer than if he'd simply had to whip a hundred turns of twine around a sapling log. The proportions were about the same, but the copper tap line was stiff, his wet fingers were slippery, and if he cut himself, he could wind up bleeding indeed when those hammerheads smelled it!

He stopped every few turns to check them out. There

was a porthole to the front and either side of the helmet, and he could of course move his head inside it. He was out of luck from the rear unless he wanted to twist his whole body at the waist. He wanted to. But each time he took time out to look the sharks over, they were still looking him over at a polite distance. He wondered what in hell they thought he was. He could only hope they wouldn't come closer to find out. Maybe he could stop one of them with his spear, but after that it would be up for grabs, with blood in the water ringing the dinner bell for sharks too far away to see!

He was almost finished when he stopped for another look-see and saw something he didn't like much. It wasn't another hammerhead. A wall of white silt was moving across the sea bottom toward him, like a fog bank. He frowned and muttered, "What the hell?" Then he went back to work. Obviously something had disturbed the bottom, a lot, up-current. But, with luck, he'd finish before the oncoming silt enveloped him. He resisted the impulse to work faster. He didn't want them to tell him he had to come back down and do it again. His mouth was dry with the green taste of fear on his tongue, but he was used to that. A knock-around guy had to keep his nerves under control and do the job right. So, he did. He finished the induction coil and secured it with a few inches of friction tape from the tool kit on his belt. Then he muttered, "Enough of this shit. Time to haul ass!"

But he rose slowly, not wanting to excite the sharks in the middle distance. The fog bank of silt was almost upon him. So, he backed toward the shadow of *Nombre Nada,* facing the milky wall. He knew anything swimming in it could see him better than he could see it, and he still didn't know who'd stirred up the silt with its tail, fins, or whatever. He doubted it was a minnow.

The first tendrils of silt enveloped Captain Gringo as he was almost under the ladder. He could still see eight or

ten feet in front of him, sort of. He forced himself to remain calm as he gripped the spear and lifeline in one hand
and reached up with his other to adjust the exhaust valve
on his helmet. He was afraid to signal the deck to haul him
in. They could do so too quickly, and he didn't want to
be trolled like a tempting bait. He knew another way to
surface. It was a bit tricky. If you inflated your suit too
much, you bobbed to the surface like a cork. If you let
the air escape faster than it was being pumped to you,
the water pressure could hug you to death, at this depth.
He wasn't far down enough to worry about the bends,
within reason, if he didn't get really silly with the pressure.
So, he adjusted the valve just a little, and sure enough, he
felt lighter and lighter and his lead soles left the bottom
as he slowly drifted upward toward safety.

Somebody skulking in the silt cloud he'd deliberately
stirred up didn't like that. So, as Captain Gringo floated
upward, he suddenly spotted something coming at him out
of the mist, fast!

There wasn't time to think. Captain Gringo thrust his
spear instinctively, and by the time he realized it was another human being, armed with a machete and naked save
for an odd, masklike triangular helmet, the butcher-knife
blade of his spear had ripped the sonofabitch open from
ribs to pubic bone, spilling his guts and a billowing cloud
of what looked like chocolate syrup between them! Captain Gringo knew that human blood wasn't red this deep
under water, but it was still blood, and a lot of it! He
gasped, "Oh boy!" and inflated his suit more to chase his
bubbles to the top. As his helmet broke the surface, he
grabbed the rungs of the ladder and started climbing. The
guys above got the message and started hauling on his
lines to help him. So, all the first hammerhead to hit him
got was the taste of metal and some loose teeth as it
snapped at Captain Gringo's left boot, a foot above the
water.

Up on deck, he sat heavily on a barrel as they started taking off his gear. Gaston, at the rail, called out, *"Merde alors!* The sharks have gone mad down there! I can't see what is going on, but it looks like someone whipping blood and milk in a bowl with fish tails. What happened, Dick?"

Captain Gringo said, "I got luckier than Carmichael. He wasn't hit by a shark. Some sonofabitch cut his air line with a machete! I was too close to the hull to try that on me. So, he took a more direct approach, and guess who won?"

"Another diver? That's incredible! From where? There is no other vessel within miles!"

"Tell me something I didn't know. Hurry it up, guys. I have to pay another social call on those innocent turtle hunters!"

As he climbed out of the suit and strapped on his gun rig again, Gaston said, "It won't work, Dick. That key is too far for anyone to swim underwater all the way. The lookout would have spotted a human head if he'd surfaced to breathe, *non?"*

"Yeah, but who looks at a shark fin in these waters? The bastard had some sort of basketwork cone over his head. Remember that so-called fin we spotted right after Carmichael bought the farm?"

"Ah, *oui,* it was headed south, toward that key, too!"

They didn't go right away. By the time Captain Gringo issued the arms and started to plan the assault, he'd had time to think. The islanders hadn't fired at them the first time because nobody but an idiot fires at anyone armed with a machine gun unless he thinks he has to. Now that Alejandro or somebody built like him had been shredded by hammerheads, the rules of the game could change. The guys on the scrub-covered key had cover.

Anyone crossing open water toward them wouldn't. So, it was literally a Mexican standoff until the sun went down again.

Obviously, the islanders didn't have the guts or muscle to assault the *Nombre Nada* openly, or they'd have done so by now. Captain Gringo decided to hit them under cover of darkness. Hard. Meanwhile, they had other chores.

He found the two girls and the two fairies busily recording messages in the salon. They seemed busy as hell. The tap was working. Clarke and Chadwick took turns fiddling with switches to amplify the eddy currents with their mysterious black boxes. Phoebe had on a set of earphones and was scribbling like hell in shorthand as the gramophone recorded anything she missed. Across the card table from her, Flora was transcribing the blonde's Spanish shorthand into English longhand and looking for hidden messages. Captain Gringo picked up a sheet of paper and read, "Sell A.B.N. Apply proceeds DuPont."

He knew who DuPont was, and anyone could see that if a real brawl broke out in Cuba, anyone making smokeless powder figured to show a profit in the near future. He didn't want to disturb the girls. But Flora noted the puzzled look on his face and took the sheet from him to reread it. She said, "A.B.N. is American Bank Notes, Incorporated, in New York. They make money printing paper money for other people."

He nodded and picked up another sheet as she went back to work. Somebody figured he was holding too much stock in an outfit that made paper money. Big deal. Both the Spanish and Cuban libs handed out pretty useless paper money. By itself, the message wasn't much more.

He'd been taught at West Point that military intelligence seldom consisted of just picking up the whole picture in one bunch of bananas. It was only in spy novels that somebody ran off with the enemy battle plans in his pocket. Any military operation called for boxes and boxes of paperwork. Spies stole a clue here and a clue there, and let the heavy thinkers topside figure out the big picture.

He read, "John Brown wants too much. Suggest Wedgwood." He caught Flora's eye and she said, "I know. It has to be a code. It makes no sense as sent. There's no way Queen Victoria's late butler and mayhaps lover could be in competition with Wedgwood China, Limited. I've put that aside to work on later."

He nodded, dropped the message on her growing pile, and stepped over to Chadwick to ask, "Are you picking up any telephone messages?"

Chadwick lisped, "No, thank heavens. Everything's in international Morse. It makes life ever so much simpler. We can record much more on a gramophone drum by speeding up the machine while recording and slowing it down for dear Phoebe to transcribe. Dots and dashes are like that."

"Military line," said Captain Gringo with a firm nod, adding, "I figured it had to be, this far south."

"The Spanish military buys Wedgwood china?"

"Why not? Everybody else does. Keep up the good work, gang."

He went back on deck to join Gaston by the bow machine gun. He'd ordered *Nombre Nada* sprung on her moorings to face the key to the south head on. Any sons-of-bitches intending a pirate dash in small craft would have their work cut out for them, rowing toward the high barricaded bluff bows instead of the lower and more open stern.

He told Gaston about the first messages, and Gaston agreed they sounded like someone was chatting in code. Captain Gringo stared westward at the pencil line Mexican coast and said, "The question before the house is, who in hell is chatting with whom? You told me there's nothing over that way but mangrove swamps."

"Mes oui. Nothing in Yucatán manages to rise more than a few feet above sea level. Since the Mayan Empire fell apart to be devoured by jungle, this has not seemed important, since hardly anyone is stupid enough to want to live in Yucatán these days."

"Okay, but if nobody's there, who's holding the mainland end of this string? The Mexican military makes little sense. The few communications in Yucatán are along the coastline to the north, right?"

"True. Why build roads or anything else through *très fatigue* jungle when there is no need to, *hein?* What Mexico calls the post road to Merida is little more than a jungle trail. From the state capital to Tizimin, the farthest town east, the post road gets worse. But it still would make more sense for them to string their communications lines along that route. There is nothing but a few isolated Indian villages due west of here, and for countless miles beyond."

Captain Gringo thought and said, "Okay. The cable could have been run down along the beach from this Tizimín, then, right?"

"Mes non. In the first place, there is no continuous beach over there. It is a disgusting line of low sea cliffs and broad, impenetrable mangrove swamps. In the second place, Tizimín is at least eighty of your English miles inland!"

"No shit? Okay, try her this way. If the nearest town Mexico knows it has is miles from here, Cuban libs must have set up a secret base in the mainland jungle where neither the *rurales* nor the Spanish army can bother them."

"It won't work. It would have to be a rebel city, not a camp, to justify this expensive undersea communication with Cuba. I repeat expensive, too! *Merde alors,* where would Cuban guerrillas get the money, or the skill, to string a cable from Mexico to Cuba?"

"From their American backers, of course. Half the

U.S. Congress is after President Cleveland to kick the Spanish out of Cuba. The Cuba Libre movement is being run from New York by Cuban exiles, and every time they pass the hat, their Yankee pals fill it up. This figures to be one of the best-financed revolutions in history. I wouldn't be surprised if the States just took off the gloves and waded into Spain personally!"

"*Sacrebleu*, whatever for?"

"Beats me. Something to do with the Spanish Armada, I guess. Spain doesn't get a favorable report in American history books. Maybe it just makes them nervous to have constant revolutions going on eighty miles south of Florida. It's been a while since I worked for the U.S. government. Let's not worry about why or what's going on. Our job's about finished here, whatever the hell it is."

"*Eh bien*, that's about the nicest thing you've said all day! How long do we have to hover over this species of mysterious cable, Dick?"

"I'm not sure. I'm still only in charge of security. I'll ask Flora tonight how much gossip Greystoke wants us to record before we can cut out. Obviously he doesn't expect us to stay here long. I get the impression the Brits are after some particular message."

Gaston glanced up at the sun. It was getting low, but not low enough. He said, "If they got it before sundown, we could spare ourselves the risk and fatigue of attacking those so-called turtle hunters, *non?*"

"No. They killed one of our people, remember?"

"*Merde alors*, I was hoping you wouldn't say that, my old and evil-tempered friend!"

Leaving Gaston in command aboard *Nombre Nada* again, Captain Gringo and a picked crew pushed off in the long-boat. He knew there were about a dozen men on the key, and the women could be tough, too. So he took away eight, dividing his forces about evenly with Gaston. He doubted that Miguelito and his lads would be surprised by their visit. But they had the darkness and hopefully superior discipline going for them. His men had been trained by the Royal Navy. God alone knew where the mealy-mouthed Miguelito and his guys had gone to school.

The machine gun he took along offered to even the odds pretty good, too.

Gaston had suggested that since he knew the lay of the land and none of it was high enough to get behind in any case, it would be most *"pratique"* simply to sweep the whole key with machine-gun fire from a safe distance and not risk a landing until everything and everybody on the key was flat.

Gaston was doubtless right. On the other hand, it seemed sort of shitty to machine gun women, and four of the gang were. He wanted a few words with someone alive in any case. So, he told his boat crew to row around the key so he could hit them from the south shore, where they'd least expect it.

By now it was black as a bitch under the trees. As the bow grated on the coral, Captain Gringo snapped, "Spread out and cover down!" as he leaped ashore with the Maxim cradled in his arms.

Nothing happened. He braced the heavy weapon on his hip with the belt trailing and started moving inland. He spotted firelight through the brush ahead and grinned wolfishly. Could old Miguelito really be dumb enough not to have guessed his game was up? Probably not. So, the tall American moved in slowly.

As he approached the camp he saw the four women and one man squatting around a small fire, talking softly among themselves. There was nobody else in view. What the hell was going on?

He took cover behind a palmetto to study his options.

One of the others joined him to whisper, "What's up, mate?"

"Shut up and move back. I'm trying to figure it out."

The one man had been with the gang during his earlier visit but hadn't said anything. Young Veronica had been sullen as hell, before. Now she looked more relaxed, and she'd combed her hair and washed her face. It was a hell of an improvement. He called out, "Hey, Veronica?" and the girl leaped a foot in the air to land facing him, eyes wary as she peered into the darkness and demanded, *"Quien es?"*

He said, "Come here. I want to talk to you. You, *hombre,* by the fire, stay put and don't do anything silly with your hands. Shake a leg, Veronica. I'm holding a gun on you."

The Mexican girl lowered her head sullenly but moved toward him. When she was close enough so that anybody shooting from behind her would hit her, he said, "It is I, the Americano called Ricardo. What's going on here? Where are the others?"

Veronica looked relieved and said, "Oh, we were wondering how to signal you without getting shot. Tio Pepe is afraid you and your friends think we are evil, like those others."

"Let's talk about those others, Veronica. Who are they and, more important, where are they?"

She said, "They left, in their sloop. We have no boat now. They chopped Tio Pepe's dugout for firewood. I don't know who they were, except that they were evil. They found us here, hunting turtles, and we have been so frightened. Tia Maria said they might not ravage me if I made myself ugly, but even so, I was afraid they would."

He called out, "Gilmore, take four men and sweep to my left. Jensen, you and the others to the right. I don't think you'll meet anybody. But if you do, shoot to kill!"

As his men moved to obey him, he grounded the heavy Maxim but remained in the shadows, .38 in hand, as he asked Veronica to fill him in some more. She told him that the man over there was her uncle and the other three women were his wives, Tia Maria, Tia Lolita, and Tia Juana. He didn't comment. He knew how many nominal Cristianos in the lowland jungles followed older Indian customs. Old Pepe wasn't a sex maniac. It made economic sense to have more than one wife down here. There were few labor-saving devices, and in any case a woman without a man to protect her was in big trouble. So, good-hearted peons tended to marry their brother's widow if nobody else would have her. Veronica's Tio Pepe had to be good-hearted indeed, when one looked at his harem. The three tias between them didn't add up to one attractive lay. Since incest was regarded with distaste in these parts, he could assume young Veronica got to sleep alone. Most Indians would rather eat a relative than sleep with one. They went further than the Catholic Church on that sin. A good Spanish Catholic was allowed to marry a distant cousin. These Maya-Mestizos wouldn't have sex with anyone who even had the same clan totem.

He questioned Veronica further, about Miguelito and his gang, not her sex life. She could tell him only that the gang had invaded them a few days back, helped themselves to their pathetic supplies, and told them to behave if they wanted to go on living. Apparently none of the women had been molested. So, the gang either shared Captain Gringo's taste in women or they'd been on serious business. Veronica verified his suspicions that the late Alejandro had been a diver, and the one he'd fed to the sharks. She said that Alejandro had dived here and there in the channel to verify the location of something. They hadn't told their unwilling hosts what. It didn't matter. Captain Gringo knew. They'd been sent here to check out the same cable. But they hadn't tried to tap it. Perhaps they'd been guarding it? That explained their desire to kill people in diving suits. But who in hell could they have been? Mexico wouldn't fool around like that. They had uniformed *rurales* to guard stuff. Cuban rebels? Possible. But if Cubans were securing their own lines of communications, why had Alejandro had to check to see that they were in place? Wouldn't he have yelled "Cuba Libre!" and *cut* the cable if the Spaniards were using it?

He decided that the only way to figure it out would be to give his decoders more time. Meanwhile, nothing interesting was going on right here. As his scouts reported in to say the whole key was deserted, Captain Gringo joined the marooned turtle hunter and his harem by the fire, with Veronica, and said, "All right, Señor Pepe, *mi casa es su casa*. I can't spare you a boat, but you're welcome to come aboard our schooner until we have time to put you ashore somewhere."

Pepe got to his feet, hat in hand, and said, *"El señor* is most kind, but we have no *dinero*. Those bad men took all we had."

"Veronica told me. Please don't think I mean to insult you by offering you food and shelter. We are all Cristianos here, no?"

"Well, my father said he was, when the *rurales* were about. My mother never got around to it."

"No matter. I won't make you pray to my gods. Naturally, you can stay here if you like, but . . ."

"We shall accept your kind offer, "Pepe cut in, adding sadly, "In God's truth, we are tired of dried turtle meat and there is nothing else to eat on this thrice accursed island!"

Nombre Nada had not been designed as a cruise ship, so after they'd fed the Mexicans, Captain Gringo had to find room for them. He couldn't put four women in the fore-castle, however much the crew might have wanted him to. The late Carmichael had rated his own private quarters, of course. So he gave Carmichael's small but private quarters to Tio Pepe and his three tias. As junior officers, the two mariposas, Clarke and Chadwick, had been quartered in private cubbyholes, too. They seemed more than willing to share one bunk. So, Captain Gringo put Veronica in Chadwick's. It was already neat and feminine. The Mexicans seemed awed by their luxurious accomodations, and the grateful Tio Pepe ordered his women to make themselves useful in all ways to the *simpatico* gringos who'd taken them in. One tia proceeded to sweep and dust everything in sight, and another joined the galley crew to scrub pots and pans, but would soon be showing them how to make tortillas. Little Veronica said she could sew. So, she went right to work mending and darning socks for anyone who needed it. As tropic Mexicans, they were of course night people and hence saw no need to go right to sleep in their new quarters.

The English aboard were getting used to working late in the cool of the tropic nights, too. So, it was after midnight when bubbly Phoebe removed her earphones in the salon and announced that no messages had come over the cable for some time. Flora said to leave the gramophone on just in case and continued to decode, or try to decode, what they'd picked up so far.

The two pansies adjusted all their dials and announced that they were ever so tired and wanted to turn in. As they left Captain Gringo and the two girls in the salon, Phoebe giggled and said, "I'll bet I know what they'll be doing for the next few hours."

Flora said, "Don't be beastly. dear. Hello, that's queer."

Phoebe said, "That's what I just said."

Flora said, "I'm not talking about the dear boys. I'm talking about the messages we intercepted before the line went dead. This is the fourth time they sent the same message about John Brown and Wedgwood. It still makes no sense to me, but it seems to be important to someone."

Captain Gringo asked, "Did anyone reply to the bit about John Brown being more reasonable than Wedgwood china?"

"I can't tell. None of the messages going the other way seem to mention either John Brown or Wedgwood. But I see two possible answers to that. The reply could have been in code, or the message could have been repeated because someone in Cuba is still waiting for an answer."

"How are you coming with your decoding, then?"

"Beastly. None of the messages seem to be in cyphers. If any contain hidden messages, they're in code."

"There's a difference?"

"Of course. A cypher is a cryptic message using different lottors or numbers to be unscrambled at the other end. A cypher usually reads like nonsense. A code is the use of whole words or phrases that mean something else. For instance, the people at both ends could agree in advance that 'Aunt Martha just died' means an arms shipment is on the way or the police are on to us."

"Gotcha. You say only that one message has been repeated more than one time? I'd concentrate on that if I were you."

Flora said, "I am," and then said, "I say!" as the schooner rose under them sickeningly.

Captain Gringo frowned and said he'd have a look. The *Nombre Nada* rocked again, hard, as he made his way topside. He joined Gaston and Rice near the binnacle and said, "We seem to be catching some ground swells tonight."

Gaston said, *"Mes oui.* Regard the stars to our east, Dick."

Captain Gringo followed Gaston's gaze and said, "I don't see any stars over that way."

"Neither do I. I told you my bones were sending me messages."

Rice said, "This channel will be a death trap if we're hit by storm winds here, look you!"

Captain Gringo wet a finger to test the breeze. There wasn't any. He said, "Oh boy! But look on the bright side. The eye of the hurricane must be miles from here. If it's due east, we have nothing to worry about. Most hurricanes track north."

Gaston snorted in disgust and said, "Except the ones who choose to track west. M'sieur Rice is right. We should consider getting some sea room, Dick."

Captain Gringo shook his head and said, "Not yet. We're hooked to the cable under us, and the girls seem to be on to something big going over the wire."

"Merde alors, the damned cable will still be there when the storm passes over. Now that you have eliminated the sea monster who killed Carmichael, how long would it take you to tap the line a second time?"

"No, thanks. The sharks in this channel have tasted human flesh and know they can find it close to this hull! It won't be safe to dive for at least a few days. I don't know how long a shark remembers a good meal, but I don't want to find out the hard way!"

The schooner bobbed sickeningly again and Rice complained, "You're going to feed us all to the sharks, look you! We're over shallow ground. The troughs between hurricane swells can bump our keel on the coral below, you see!"

"Oh, for God's sake, Rice, these swells are widely spaced and not more than six feet from trough to crest. I'm not about to stay here in this channel if there's a real blow. But let's not wet our pants until we know one's heading our way, huh? The eye could pass us miles from here. It's more likely to hit Cuba than us."

Gaston sniffed, smelled nothing but brine and kelp,

and said, *"Eh bien,* in that case wake me when it's over. Since I see the stubborn set to your jaw, I shall ride the waves more comfortably in my snug, petite bunk. Ah, did the girls say what time they would be quitting for the night, Dick?"

"Why don't you just start without her if she's late in joining you, you old goat. I'll stand watch until the next one's due."

Rice said that in that case, he'd turn in too. So, they left him alone in the cockpit, sniffing for brass and hoping not to see any green stars in the near future. As he lit a Claro he noticed there was a slight breeze now. It was headed the wrong way, out to sea. But it wasn't strong, and, what the hell, the hurricane eye had a right to suck air out of Mexico, as long as it didn't overdo it.

He was getting used to the ground swell now. It was no worse than if they'd been out on the open sea on a fair day. But something sure was going on over to the east. Could that account for the cable down there going dead? Cubans were night people, too. Undersea cables were supposed to be immune from storm waves. On the other hand, they had to come out of the water somewhere, and a real storm pounding the Cuban coast could have broken the line. The only way they'd know for sure would be to wait and see if any more messages came over the line in the next twenty-four hours. Meanwhile, there was nothing to do but sweat it all out.

He'd finished his smoke and tossed the butt overboard when the seaman assigned the next watch came on deck to relieve Rice and naturally took over from Captain Gringo. The tall American went below to rejoin the girls. He found Flora alone at her card table. Flora said that Phoebe had gone to bed, or someone's bed. Captain Gringo looked down at the untidy pile of shorthand notes the blonde had left and said, "She must have been very sleepy."

Flora chuckled and replied, "She sounded very sleepy. Poor Gaston. What do you suppose Clarke and Chadwick do when they're alone, Dick?"

"I've wondered about that. Never had the nerve to ask a guy like that to let me watch."

"Phoebe says she's sure they suck each other. From the way poor little Chadwick walks, I'd say it goes deeper than that."

"Who cares? I've been thinking about that repeated message. There's more than one John Brown, isn't there? What if we forgot Queen Vickie's notorious butler and thought about other John Browns? I know it can't be the John Brown who lies a-moldering in his grave. So who's left? I seem to recall a British company called John Brown, Limited."

Flora gasped and said, "My God, of course! John Brown, Limited, is one of the biggest armor-plate producers in the U.K.! They roll steel for battleships! But that still leaves us with Wedgwood. You don't armor a cruiser with Wedgwood plates. They must mean someone else."

He nodded and said, "How about Woodbine Arms? That's pretty close, and the owner, Sir Basil Hakim, does overcharge for the arms he supplies damned near anybody with cash."

Flora nodded and said, "It fits. I've heard of Hakim. He's a bad one, even if he does drink with the Prince of Wales. But why do they keep sending the same message, Dick?"

"Ask them. If you want an educated guess, it could be the only real message they've been sending. All the other stock quotations could be just a smoke screen. We know it's a private line. Someone in Cuba is trying to contact someone on the mainland to our west. The cable under us might not hook in to the regular Mexican communications at all. From what Gaston tells me about the jungle country between here and more civilized parts, the cable may only run a few miles inland to some base nobody's supposed to know about. The messages at one end may be being recorded on a gramophone and picked up only when no *rurales* or Cuban-Spanish cops are in the neighborhood. Can you kids tell if that repeated message is being sent to or from Cuba, Flora?"

"Not really. When you listen in on a line, you have to guess from the context who's sending from each end. Why?"

"Someone in Mexico could be advising either side in Cuba that they'll get a better deal from John Brown on armor plate than they would from Hakim. Or, someone in Cuba wants to order plate and . . . Hmm."

"Hmm what, dear?"

"The Cuba Libre movement is well financed, but I can't see Cuban rebels buying battleship plates. It takes four years to build a battleship. On the other hand, Spain already has a navy."

"Wouldn't it take them four years to build new ships, too?"

"They don't have to. They already have 'em. They can't be worried about guerrillas shooting up even an antique battle wagon. But the Spanish navy is getting a little long in the tooth, and they may be worried about folks with more modern warships."

"Like the U.S.?"

"That'd be my first choice. The Monroe Doctrine reserves the right of serious warfare in this neck of the woods to Uncle Sam. So, if Spain is beefing up its old battle wagons, Spain is worried about more than guerrillas shouting Cuba Libre! Damn, to think I spent four years at the Point and now I'll be left out of the first decent war my generation will ever see!"

"You might see another in your time if that nasty young kaiser has his way. But let's stick to here and now, dear.

Obviously there isn't going to be a Spanish-American War for a few years, at the rate things are going. Do you think we can assume the cable under us is Spanish-operated?"

"It's starting to look like it. How many Cuban guerrillas could be playing the international stock market or ordering armor plate?"

"*If* it's not all in code we've yet to break, you mean. Why would the Spanish military government want to set up clandestine communications with the mainland, Dick?"

"To keep them clandestine, of course. Greystoke and the U.S. Secret Service are monitoring the obvious cable from Cuba to Florida. Give Butcher Weyler credit for knowing that. *El Presidente* Diaz would double-cross his own father, if he knew who his father was. If I were Weyler and wanted to wire secret messages, I think we're tapped in to how I'd go about it. He can send anything he likes on this private line to agents in Mexico. They in turn can relay them to Spain or whatever."

"That makes sense. But what does all this mean to British Intelligence, Dick? Even if that business about armor plate is true and not a code for something else, why should Whitehall care? The British navy isn't about to get into a brawl with either Spain or the U.S. in the near future."

He shrugged and said, "I guess London just likes to keep posted. Any battleship war, anywhere, would be of interest to the R.N., I guess. Are you about through here?"

She smiled up at him and said, "I was hoping you'd suggest that, dear." So, he pulled her to her feet and kissed her. But as they headed for his stateroom the *Nombre Nada* rolled sickeningly, and Flora asked, "Do you expect this storm to get worse, Dick?"

He said, "It's not a storm yet. The deck watch will let us know if we can't guess by the way she's rocking. Meanwhile, we won't notice the roll as much in bed, right?"

They got to his quarters. He frowned as he saw light under the door. He opened the door to see blond bubbly Phoebe reclining on the bunk, on top of the covers, stark naked. He shoved Flora inside and hastily shut the door and bolted it before he asked the blonde, "What happened? Did you lose your way, Phoebe?"

Phoebe roguishly smiled up at them and said, "Gaston's busy. I abso-bloody-lutely refuse to go three in a bed with that unwashed Tia Juana. She smells like codfish."

Flora laughed and said, "Oh, dear," as she reached for her own buttons. But Captain Gringo didn't think it was funny. He scowled and said, "My God! Gaston's in bed with one of that Mexican's wives? Gaston must have gone nuts! I'd better throw cold water over them before Tio Pepe finds out!"

Phoebe said, "Not to worry. Tio Pepe knows. He and Gaston worked out one of those *pratique* arrangements dirty old men go in for. It seems Tio Pepe feels too old to service three women every night, and . . ."

"Gotcha." Captain Gringo laughed, adding, "Tia Juana's the youngest of the three, too. Though that's not saying much."

By this time Flora had slipped out of her tropic linens and joined Phoebe, naked, on the bunk. The contrast of their two completely different bodies was interesting indeed, but Captain Gringo felt a little confused as to the ground rules. Flora laughed and said, "Everyone seems to be fixed up for the night except that poor little Veronica. She must feel terribly left out."

Phoebe said, "I say, why don't we invite her to join our orgy?"

Captain Gringo said, "Oh, right, we're having an orgy. I was starting to wonder what the hell was going on. I think we'd better leave Veronica to her own devices. I'm not sure I can handle the bounty I'm about to receive!"

He snuffed out the lamp. He felt silly undressing in front of both of them, for some reason. He'd had them both. But they were still making him feel shy as they exchanged clinical comments about his body, like naughty school chums rapping about sex in the dorm.

He climbed in with them, gathered female curves in each arm, and muttered, "Decisions, decisions! You sure have gotten over your shyness, Flora."

Flora grasped his shaft and toyed with it as she purred, "I don't have to worry about becoming a lesbian if I'm in bed with a man, do I?"

"That's one way of looking at it. Who goes first?"

"Oh, why don't you fuck Phoebe first? We want to try something new."

That sounded reasonable. He'd had Flora most recently. Phoebe laughed and rolled on her hands and knees to present her upthrust rump. There was just enough light coming through the door cracks from the companionway for him to see what he was doing as he rose to the occasion, both ways, and entered her from the rear, standing barefoot on the floor. As he felt himself in her softer blond body he growled, "Oh, yeah!" and started humping. He assumed Flora would heat up nicely as she watched. But the girls had been talking together indeed. As he rutted with Phoebe dog style, Flora slid her naked spine along the bulkhead until she was in line with Phoebe's blond head, thighs wide. Phoebe dropped her face in Flora's lap and proceeded to eat her as she was being stimulated more properly at her other end. Captain Gringo blinked in surprise but kept servicing the blonde. He couldn't have stopped, and it did seem to add a certain spice to the proceedings. Flora liked it, too. She leaned her brunette head back against the bulkhead, eyes closed, and gasped as she said, "Oh, my God, that does feel marvelous!"

As long as they were being clinical, Captain Gringo

chuckled and said, "I thought you didn't go in for that sort of thing, Flora."

The girl being eaten replied, "I don't. I'm not the one being queer. I'm not sure dear Phoebe's really being queer, when one considers what a man is doing to her at the moment. I'd ask her, but I don't want her to stop!"

The combination of perverse and old fashioned sex seemed to be driving Phoebe wild, too, to judge from her internal contractions. She suddenly stiffened her legs, ejecting him like a wet watermelon seed as she rolled over on her back, gasping. "I can't stand any more! I've come twice and I'm too excited to live! I have to take time out to get hold of myself!"

That left both the man she'd been screwing and the girl she'd been eating up in the air, literally. So Captain Gringo grabbed Flora's legs, pulled her closer, and dropped into her saddle. She was panting with passion and gushing with desire, and her love maw felt so different around his shaft that he came almost at once. She did, too, screaming aloud in pure animal pleasure.

He whispered, "Hey, keep it down to a roar!"

Flora said, "I'm so excited! Turn me over and shove it in my bum!"

"Are you sure you want that, doll?"

"Yes, I want to be low and dirty and wild, now that I've begun to learn how nice it can be!"

He grimaced, but it was her ass they were talking about, and he wanted to be a sport. So, he got to his feet again, pulled her into position, and gingerly worked his moist love tool into her pulsing anal opening as she beat on the mattress with her fists and hissed, "Oh, Jesus, that feels so strange! Are you sure a girl can come this way, Phoebe?"

Phoebe rolled under her, apparently recovered, and said, "Anyone can come anytime, with a little help from a friend!"

So, as Captain Gringo sodomized Flora, Phoebe began to lick her clit from below. Her blond hair tickled Captain Gringo's legs as it hung, bobbing, between them. Flora gasped, "Oh, loverly!" as she crouched, with her spine arched, her face above the saucy blonde's open thighs. It took her a while to get up the nerve. But Captain Gringo wasn't really surprised when she suddenly giggled, took a deep breath, and began to return Phoebe's favor with her own questing tongue. He shook his head and marveled, "Boy, talk about orgies!" And then, since everybody had everything important taken care of, all three of them proceeded to come together. They wound up in a tangled pile on the bunk. His dick was in somebody. It didn't matter who, or where. He just kept moving as they both took turns kissing him. But just as he was almost there again, he heard the deck watch call out. He couldn't hear the words, but it sounded important. He untangled himself from the two crazy little dames and rolled out of the love pile, saying, "Be right back. Gotta see what's up."

What was up, when he went up on deck with his pants and gun on, was apparently the wind. The sailor said, "I saw a light off to the west, captain. It's gone now."

"That's the Mexican coast over that way. Did it look like a signal?"

"I don't know, captain. It was just a light. It blinked on and off. One time."

Captain Gringo shrugged and said, "Probably a Mexican going somewhere with a lantern. People do that at night, you know."

"I thought the jungles over there were deserted, sir."

"*Deserted* is a relative term. *Chicleros* wander through the trees looking for chewing gum for Mr. Wrigley. Others gather Spanish moss, rubber, stuff like that. Some peons even do a little slash-and-burn farming in the Yucatán lowlands. Keep an eye peeled, of course. But let's not cry wolf unless we really see one, eh? Keep up the good work I'm going back to bed."

He went below again. When he got to his quarters, Flora and Phoebe were going sixty-nine and seemed unaware of him as he watched for a time, muttered, "Oh, shit," and stepped back out in the companionway. He felt pretty well sated for the moment, and, in truth, the two English girls were overdoing things a bit for his taste. Bubbly blond Phoebe was a pretty little amoral moron, and Flora was just weird. He still liked them both. He'd doubtless wind up laying both again. But for some reason, at the moment, the game was getting a bit rich for his romantic nature.

He decided to take an inspection tour as long as he was out here. He'd told his crew to secure everything that could come loose in a storm, but you never knew.

He went into the salon. The lamp was lit and the battery-driven gramophone was hissing quietly as it recorded silence. He picked up Phoebe's earphones and had a listen. Nothing. Her shorthand notes were on the floor now. As he bent to pick them up, he saw others in the wastebasket under the table. He picked out a dozen sheets of foolscap at random, folded them, and put them in his hip pocket. He wasn't sure why. But he could read shorthand, and he was beginning to wonder if the girls told him everything. They'd obviously had some discussions in private, earlier, and while some surprises were sure fun, others might not be.

He went down to the engine room. Nobody was on duty, but the pilot light was on under the boiler. They could get up steam within an hour if need be. So, there was nothing for him to do there.

He didn't go to the forecastle or the galley. He didn't want to ask the crew anything, and he was tired of telling them not to worry. He didn't want to try brewing coffee with the fucking tub rolling like this, either. His smokes and other pleasures were back in his quarters. So, he headed back to them. Now that he'd recovered his second wind, there seemed to be something to be said for this orgy business after all. He laughed and murmured, "Decisions, decisions!" as he tried to decide whose turn it was.

He passed Gaston's door. He listened. He heard exactly what he expected to hear. He grinned and moved on to where Clarke and Chadwick were sharing a bunk. They were still at it, whatever it was. He couldn't picture what was going on in there, but it sounded like a lot of work.

He wasn't expecting to hear anything from Veronica's cubbyhole. But as he passed her door he heard the sounds of sobbing. Tio Pepe and his two tias were just snoring next door, so that couldn't be it. He rapped gently. Veronica gasped and went silent as a church mouse.

Not wanting either to attract attention or to abandon the kid to whatever misery she was obviously feeling, he tried the latch. It was unlocked. He opened the door and murmured, "It is I, Ricardo. What's the matter, *querida?*"

Veronica lay under a sheet, apparently naked. She said, "I am not your *querida*. I am nobody's *querida*. I am almost seventeen and everybody thinks I'm ugly."

He stepped inside and sat on the edge of her bunk before he said soothingly, "I don't think you're ugly. I find you very beautiful."

It was a white lie. Her little moon face was okay, now that she'd washed it. Her figure was better than okay. But she was probably a virgin, so what the hell. He asked, "Why are you crying? Has anyone been cruel to you aboard this vessel?"

"Of course not. Everyone has been *muy simpatico*. I am afraid because I think we are going to sink. A hurricane is coming. I can feel it."

"You too? The storm won't hit for hours, even if it's

headed this way. If it really gets bad, we'll head out to sea where we'll be safe. Why don't you try to get some sleep, eh?"

But as he started to rise, Veronica sat up, exposing her muskmelon-shaped brown breasts as she pleaded, "Don't go! I do not wish to be alone. I am frightened, Señor Ricardo. Stay here and comfort me. Stay here and perhaps hold me in your strong Yankee arms? I do not think I would feel so frightened if you were here to protect me."

He took the little Mestiza in his arms. As soon as he felt her warm brown flesh against his bare chest, he knew he might have made a mistake. But, hell, it wasn't as if he was hard up. He had plenty of the real thing waiting for him in his own bunk. So, he told his love tool to behave its fool self as he cuddled the frightened girl and said, "I'll stay with you a little while."

"A little while? Can't you stay the night? There is plenty of room for two in this luxurious grand bed, no?"

He smiled down at her and said, "It's a little seaman's bunk, and I'm not all that noble, either. I'm trying to feel brotherly, Veronica. But it's not easy. Has anyone ever told you you have great little tits?"

She snuggled closer and said, "Of course. Lots of boys have wished to feel them. But, alas, nobody has ever asked me to marry them afterwards."

He laughed and said, "I can't get married. I took a vow. But I'd better get out of here pronto, if you don't want to include me in your list of afterwards, kitten."

She answered, innocent as a child, "Oh, do you wish to make love to me? I think I would like that very much, Señor Ricardo."

He started to tell her not to be silly. Then he wondered who was being silly in here. The latch was locked, the other girls were busy, this one was rubbing her nipples all over him, so what the hell!

He laughed and said, "You're on," as he slipped off his

pants, pulled the sheet out of the way, and simply mounted her like an old pal. As he settled into the saddle between her strong brown thighs, he noticed that, like many Indian women, she was hairless down there. That wasn't the only pleasant contrast he felt as he entered her. She gasped and said, "Oh, you are so *muy toro!* But why do you say *I* am on? It is you who is on me, no?" He didn't answer. He was busy. As she started to move with strong, natural thrusts of her childlike pubis, she sighed and said he was the biggest man she'd ever had in there. He believed her. She was tighter than hell, and most Indian or part-Indian men in this part of Mexico were hung sort of small, God bless them. He could tell she was part Maya. He'd had Mayan girls before. If the Mayan Empire had crumbled because of a low birth rate, as some said, it had obviously been the fault of the men. Their women were hot as hell.

She seemed willing, but she refused to be kissed as he made love to her. So, he didn't suggest anything acrobatic. There was no need to. Veronica was just a sweet, old-fashioned lay. So, he layed her until she'd come twice to his once. Then they just lay there contented in each other's arms. It felt good to be with a plain, uncomplicated peon woman again.

They made love one more time before she fell asleep in his arms. He gently slid out of the bed and hauled his pants back on. Not because he wanted to rejoin the orgy in his own quarters. He didn't think he could get it up again. He went back topside because the schooner was really starting to fight her anchor now. The surf was getting rougher by the minute.

He found Gaston and half the crew on deck. The wind was from the west and rising. He nodded at Gaston and said, "Great minds run in the same channels, eh?"

"Merde alors, this channel is not a place to ride out a

hurricane! We have to abandon our cable tap and get some deep water under our keel!"

Captain Gringo nodded but said, "Yes and no. We can unreel our tap wire as we go ashore."

"*Sacrebleu,* we are going ashore?"

Some of us have to, Gaston. If we set up our listening post over on the north key, the guys aboard can take *Nombre Nada* out to sea to ride out the storm, then come back to pick us up when it's over."

"North key? Don't you mean the south key, where we picked up the Mexicans? That key to the north is even more barren, Dick!"

"I noticed. It's more barren because it's higher above the water and almost solid rock. We'll be safer there. Let's not debate it. Let's get moving. We have to put the listening gear and supplies for a few days ashore while we can still keep the longboat afloat in these waves!"

Gaston shook his head stubbornly and said, "Talk sense, Dick! What if something happens to this schooner? We'd wind up marooned, no?"

"I guess so. On the other hand, do you really want to be aboard if the *Nombre Nada* sinks?"

"Well, since you put it that way, why are we wasting time discussing the matter? Let us get the crack, as you Yankees say, *hein?*"

An hour later, Captain Gringo, Gaston, the two English girls, and their two swishy friends had set up their shore base on the barren north key. He'd suggested that the Mexicans stay with the others aboard *Nombre Nada,* where they'd be safer. But Tio Pepe was afraid to get any farther away from his native Mexico than he and his women already were. So, they chose to join the shore party.

By then the wind was really blowing. So, *Nombre Nada* weighed anchor and let the offshore wind take her out to sea, moving pretty good, with her poles bare and her engine at half-speed holding her bow to the waves coming in against the wind. The castaways began to feel mighty lonely, even before their only link with civilization vanished in the howling night.

It got worse before morning. No waves actually broke completely over their little dot of dry land. But some of the waves came mighty high, and the land didn't stay dry. There was no hope of erecting a shelter that wouldn't just blow away. So, they lashed their gear to the few tree trunks, lashed themselves as well, and simply waited it out. Naturally, nobody thought about food, sleep, or sex while frog-sized raindrops hopped all over them. The night was a long, unpleasant experience.

But by dawn the winds had shifted around to the northeast again, and as the sun rose with the trades behind it, it promised to be a fine clear day after all. The surf was still rolling ominously all around them, but, as Captain Gringo had hoped, they'd been spared the eye of the hurricane, and as it tracked north to bother other people, even the sea began to settle down.

The Mexican women built a fire and proceeded to make tortillas from the flour in the supply cases they'd landed. The English girls and the two mariposas got back on the line. But, even though the tap was still firmly attached to the cable out in mid-channel, nothing was being sent from either end. Clarke tested the current and said, "I think the cable must have been broken by the storm. We've stranded ourselves here for nothing!"

Captain Gringo said, "Quit your bitching. Like I said, if the schooner's still afloat, they'll be back in a while to pick us up. If it's not, you have only me to thank."

They ate and dried out. They dried out more than they really needed to as the morning wore on. Captain Gringo and Gaston rigged sunshades between the palmettos with canvas tarps. So, they managed to stay out of the direct rays of the sun, at least, but it still got hotter and hotter by the hour.

They were all feeling wilted and listless by three. But Gaston had to take a leak anyway. He left to find some bushes. When he came back, he dropped on the white sand beside Captain Gringo and·said, "We have company. I just spotted a sail to the south. At the moment it is behind that other key."

Captain Gringo told the others to lie low as he rose and moved to the highest ground on the key, which meant only a few paces. Gaston joined him just as the shark-fin sails of a low-slung Carib rounded the south key, headed their way. Gaston said, "That does not look like the *Nombre Nada* to me, Dick!"

Captain Gringo called Tio Pepe to join them. The old turtle hunter nodded and said, "*Sí,* that is the evil boat of that *ladrón,* Miguelito! But why have they returned?"

Captain Gringo said, "Easy. They saw *Nombre Nada* was gone. That was the light our watch spotted last night, and I owe that guy an apology! They're not just *ladrónes,* Pepe. Somebody's paid them to keep an eye on things here!"

"What shall we ever do, Captain Gringo?"

As Captain Gringo moved back to their piled supplies and pulled the tarp off the one machine gun they'd brought ashore, Gaston told Pepe, "That is what he's going to do. Find some cover and stay there. They may have this key down as deserted. If they decide to recheck, ooh-la-la!"

Miguelito did. As the castaways watched, trying to remain invisible, the primitive sailboat came on bold as brass. Captain Gringo crouched behind the Maxim, coaxing, "Come on, guys. You can do it. Just a little closer, you motherfuckers!"

Gaston said, "Try to spare the hull, Dick. We may need that boat."

Captain Gringo did. But as he didn't want to let them hit the beach and fan out, he opened fire as the Carib's bow slid up on the beach like a crocodile's snout. The results were predictably messy.

The stream of machine-gun lead raked the Carib and everything in it from stem to stern, blowing some of Miguelito's crew overboard and others who got wedged in his fire to bloody hash. Gaston punched his arm and called out, "Enough! They're all down and you are chewing up the boat!"

Captain Gringo ceased fire. They waited, and, sure enough, Gaston was right. The stern of the Carib was under water, riddled with bullet holes, and nobody was moving out there. Captain Gringo said, "Cover me," and drew his .38 to survey the results.

Old Miguelito and two other guys lay in the bloody water of the half-sunken carib. They were never going to bother anybody again. Over the side, in the shallows, a wounded man was trying to flipper himself up on the beach like a wounded sea lion. So, Captain Gringo waded out, grabbed a fistful of hair, and hauled him ashore. Then he kicked him in the side to gain his full attention and snapped, "Who were you guys watching that cable for? Talk, pronto, or I feed you to the sharks!"

The shot-up *ladrón* gasped and said, "Don't hurt me, for the love of God! I will tell you anything, but please don't hurt me! I need a doctor!"

"I noticed. Who sent you guys?"

"I do not know his name. A *muy* important person Miguelito has worked for in the past. We were told to make sure nobody listened in on the telegraph cable out there. Alejandro killed one diver who did. They were on a big schooner. I swear I do not know who they were."

"No problem. I do. Just lie there and soak up some

healing rays while I see if any of you other sonsofbitches are alive."

There were no other survivors, and when he got back to the wounded man, he wasn't wounded anymore. He was dead. Captain Gringo nodded and said, "That's that, then. You can all come out now, kiddies. The party's over."

So everybody had a look at the mess, and then, since it was hot as hell and nothing seemed to be happening worth frying one's brains for, everyone but Gaston went back to the shade. Gaston waded out to examine the boat. He rejoined Captain Gringo and muttered, "Now you've done it. I could probably patch it up enough to float, but I am not about to trust my life to that hull on the open sea!"

"Relax. *Nombre Nada* ought to be back anytime now. There's not room enough for all of us and our gear in that tub in any case."

"You and I could be *pratique, non?*"

"Gee, that's what I like about you, Gaston. You're so fucking loyal!"

"*Merde alors,* loyalty stops well this side of suicide, my idealistic youth! Besides, what loyalty do we owe anyone here? We were dragooned into this foolish mission in the first place."

"Well, you may be right about it being foolish. Grey-stoke sure went to a lot of trouble to find out so little. But that's his problem. Let's get out of this sun."

They rejoined the others. Chadwick said something dumb about burying the dead. Captain Gringo said, "The rising tide will take care of 'em. Have you picked up anything from the cable yet?"

Clarke said, "There's no sign of any current at all. Do you suppose our induction coil could have come loose out there?"

Captain Gringo took hold of the insulated line, hauled

in until it was taut, and said, "I don't think so. Since the diving gear's aboard *Nombre Nada,* there's no way I'm about to find out for sure. But it feels okay. There was nothing else along that stretch of cable for the tap to snag on, and it's still attached to some damned thing."

After that, things got even duller. Gaston offered to clean the Maxim. Captain Gringo smoked a cigar and read Phoebe's shorthand notes. He saw that she'd been telling it like it was and most of the good parts were still in the wastebasket aboard *Nombre Nada.* There was nothing about John Brown and Wedgwood here. When she saw what he was doing and asked why, he told her he didn't have anything else to read. She suggested a walk to the far end of the key. He told her not to be silly. Flora pondered aloud the meanings of the messages intercepted so far, but since her notebook was on the schooner, too, he told her not to be silly either.

The castaways lapsed into silent suffering. As the sun sank to the west, it slanted in under the awnings. But, mercifully, the trades were picking up and it was getting a little cooler. Somebody asked if he thought they were stuck here for another night and he said they probably were. He didn't want to talk about the supply situation. They had plenty of food. But when he opened the case he thought was filled with water bottles, he saw that some dumb sonofabitch had put a case of dynamite ashore instead. He had enough H.E. to blow up the whole place. But they were going to be in bad shape for water in a day or so. He cursed himself for not having thought to catch some rainwater during the storm. But who thought of things like that when he thought he had a whole damned case of bottled water?

He fell asleep for a while. He didn't feel any better when Gaston woke him. But when Gaston said why, Captain Gringo was wide awake.

Off to the east, pink in the slanting sunlight, stood a

trim steam yacht. It was a big one. The owner either had a glandular problem or a lot of money. The flag flapping over the stern was British. In these waters that didn't mean a lot. So, Captain Gringo got back behind his machine gun as a longboat from the mysterious vessel headed their way.

The wrecked Carib and its crew had floated away on the prevailing current during the turn of the tide. The tide was ebbing again, so there was nothing blocking his field of fire as he covered the longboat. As it got closer, he spotted a familar figure, a grotesque one, standing in the bows like Columbus searching for the Indies. It was their old pal, Sir Basil Hakim, in the flesh. Captain Gringo knew that the dwarfish old Turk, or whatever in hell he was, seldom led a group personally unless it was very important to Woodbine Arms, Limited.

Gaston recognized their visitor at about the same time and muttered, *"Sacre* God damn! So he does make Wedgwood plates! Could I change places with you, Dick? I've always wanted to shoot that species of insect!"

Captain Gringo said, "Man the Maxim and cover me. But let's not shoot him till we see what he wants."

Captain Gringo warned the others to lie low as well. Then he stepped out in view, strode down to the water's edge, and called out, "Ahoy, Hakim! What the fuck do you want?"

Sir Basil peered his way, shielding his goatlike face with a hand. Then he called back, "Is that you, Captain Gringo? I say, this *is* jolly luck! You have your friend Gaston covering me, of course?"

"Of course. What have you got trained on us?"

Hakim laughed boyishly and replied, "A twenty-millimeter deck gun out there, naturally. But why are we threatening each other, dear boy? You know I'm an honest businessman, not a brawler. May I come ashore so we can talk like gentlemen?"

"You're full of shit about being honest or a gentleman, but, yeah, come on in and name your pleasure. It's only fair to warn you I don't bend over."

Hakim laughed, ordered his boat crew to run the bow up on the coral, and leaped ashore lightly.

Sir Basil Hakim was either a Turk, a Jew, a Russian, or perhaps a Greek, depending on whom your informant hated most. Somehow, sometime, he'd become a British subject and made so much money the queen had to knight him. The Merchant of Death was just too tall to call a dwarf but too short to call a full-grown man. Nobody knew for sure when he'd been born in Constantinople, Moscow, Berlin, or somewhere. So he could have been a seventy-year-old man who took good care of himself or a man of forty who'd ruined his looks by dissipation and degeneracy.

His hair and Buffalo Bill mustache and goatee were lavender white, and he wore French perfume, too. His elfin features wore the expression of a depraved Santa Claus as he held out a hand and said, "So good to see you again, Captain Gringo. You know why I'm here, of course."

Captain Gringo ignored the hand; he didn't want to catch anything. He nodded and said, "Yeah, I just shot the shit out of those *ladrónes* you had watching the cable until you could get here."

"Did you indeed? Pity. Oh, well, it saves my having to pay Miguelito and his lot off. Do you want to deal, Dick?"

"Maybe. What are you offering us?"

"Your lives, to begin with. You know I'm a peaceful chap at heart."

Captain Gringo smiled crookedly and said, "Right. You want a piece of everything. Our lives are in pretty good shape for the moment. Suppose you tell me exactly what you want?"

Hakim nodded and said, "Information. As you know,

Woodbine Arms, Limited, has a finger in many a pie, and as an honest businessman I like to keep informed. I have agents of my own in both Cuban camps. I have my own taps on the communications lines I already knew about. I understand our old chum Greystoke learned of a hitherto unknown cable and sent you lot to tap it. I want to listen in. I'm *going* to listen in, even if it means I have to be rude to old comrades in arms."

Captain Gringo didn't answer as he thought. The cable seemed to be dead in the water. Not even Greystoke could expect them to hang around until it was repaired, and they had a few tidbits of information London might be interested in. It was up to Whitehall whether Woodbine Arms sold armor plate to anybody or not. Since Hakim was said to supply the Prince of Wales with booze and dancing girls, they'd probably let him.

Hakim grew impatient and said, I'd like your answer, Captain Gringo."

The American looked down at him and said, "Okay. We have a line running to the cable out in mid-channel. They don't seem to be sending anything today, but you never know. Suppose we turn over our listening gear to you and call it a day? What do we get out of it?"

"My word that you and your people are free to leave, alive and unmolested."

Captain Gringo knew Hakim's word was good. The little monster could swat almost anyone like a fly, and feel as much remorse. But Hakim dealt for high stakes in a business where his word had to mean something. Ergo, if the Merchant of Death gave you his word, you could count on it. Contrarywise, if you broke your word to him or lied to him, all bets were off and he'd have his agents track you to the ends of the earth. He was one dangerous little sonofabitch to deal with. But Captain Gringo had learned in the past that it could be done.

He said, "Not good enough. Like I said, we're forted

up pretty good, and you know Gaston and I can take pretty good care of our lives. I want more."

"Oh? Well, since you've helped me economize by reducing my payroll, I suppose I could sweeten the pot. How much do you want for turning this listening post over to me and mine, Dick?"

"Two things. I sent my schooner out to the high seas to ride out that storm. They'll be coming back anytime now. I want your word you won't smoke them up."

"Agreed. How will I know this schooner? Other chaps may stick their noses in my business, and, as I said, I have a twenty-millimeter deck gun to deal with trespassers."

"My vessel's the *Nombre Nada*. You know her, of course?"

"Naturally. Esperanza and I are old business associates. Is she aboard?"

"No. British crew. You hail them, tell them we've left, and say I said they're to report back to Greystoke in Belize."

"That sounds reasonable. You said there were two conditions?"

"Yeah. We want a ride to Belize, too. You can't make a landing here unless we let you. On the other hand, we're marooned with no way to reach the mainland. Can do?"

Hakim smiled impishly and said, "You should have told me sooner. I could just let you die of hunger and thirst, you know."

"I know. But it would take us a long time, and meanwhile we'd mess up the tapping gear so you'd have to start from scratch. How long were you figuring on hanging around here, Hakim? We saw a Mexican gunboat the other day."

Hakim nodded and said, "I admire a chap who thinks on his feet. Very well, you turn over this listening post to me, in good repair. I agree not to harm any of your people and to put you and your party safely ashore on the mainland."

"Not Belize?"

"Too far, dear boy. There's a little Mexican port called Vigia Chico just down the coast. I'll land you and your luggage safely there, with Miguelito's back wages to sweeten the pot."

Captain Gringo scowled and said, "You call that safe? Gaston and I are wanted dead or alive in Mexico, pal!"

"Piffle. Vigia Chico has no direct communications with Mexico City. I don't know if there's a *rurale* station there. But, knowing you, I can only hope for their sake there isn't any. There's a rail line running back into the bush from Vigia Chico, but it doesn't go anywhere. Just to the local plantations. They grow bananas, I believe. There's no Mexican army or navy post there. There are any number of fishing boats or even coastal schooners one can either hire or highjack. How do you like it so far?"

It stinks. Can't you even ferry us to the border of British Honduras?"

"No. The run to Vigia Chico will already tie up my steam launch for a full day. I'm being very generous, Dick. If you won't settle for half a loaf, we'll just have to do things the hard way here."

Captain Gringo hesitated, nodded, and said, "Okay. Toss in a thousand extra for Gaston and I, and you've got a deal."

"A thousand extra? My, aren't we greedy? I told you I'd give you poor Miguelito's finder's fee."

"That goes to some Mexicans I rescued from Miguelito. He stripped them of their few belongings. Greystoke can pay off the Brits. He may pay us off, and then, again, you know Greystoke. Gaston and I get a grand, U.S."

Hakim didn't answer as his cash-register eyes went click click click. Captain Gringo took out Phoebe's shorthand notes and said, "You get these, too. I told you the cable's gone dead. These are messages we intercepted. I'd say they were worth a grand, to a businessman."

"What do they say?"

"Beats me. They're probably in code. We haven't decoded them."

"I have your word on that?"

"You do. None of us have any idea who laid that cable or what the messages we intercepted really meant. If I give these notes to you, we'll never know. We can't decode them if you have them, right?"

Strictly speaking, all this was true. He saw no reason to tell the sonofabitch that Flora still had her notebook transcribed into longhand, and seven or eight times more complete, nor that the discarded shorthand scraps contained nothing about John Brown, Limited.

Hakim reached in his jacket, took out a huge wad of bank notes, and peeled off a thousand dollars. He held them out to Captain Gringo and said, "Agreed." So Captain Gringo gave him Phoebe's notes and asked, "When do we leave?"

The tiny port of Vigia Chico, Quintana Roo Territory, was exactly as the Merchant of Death had promised. Nothing much. Hakim's steam launch deposited them on the quay after sunset and headed back with no further ceremony. The populace was of course wide awake and would be so until at least 3:00 A.M. So, the few streetlights were burning, the waterfront *fondas* and cantinas were open for business, and business looked slow.

As the castaways sat on their piled belongings, pondering their next move, a delegation headed by the alcalde and a local padre approached them cautiously. The alcalde removed his sombrero and said, "Welcome, good people. I hope you have been sent by the central government. It is many days since we sent runners through the jungle to get help. We were afraid they had not gotten through."

Captain Gringo kept his face blank as he replied, "Really? Who might have stopped them and why were they running?"

"*El* señor does not know about Bocanegro and his army?"

"No. Tell me about them."

The alcalde looked confused and crestfallen. The padre said, "Bocanegro calls himself a *generale*. He says he has risen against Diaz to liberate us. He says he has freed us from Mexico forever. In God's truth, that would not be such a bad idea. But Bocanegro is no liberator. He is a *ladrón!*"

"There's a lot of that going around in Mexico, padre."

"Alas, that is true. But Bocanegro is here, and those other *ladrónes* in the city of Mexico are so far away they seldom bother us. Bocanegro makes us pay tribute to him. Impossible tribute. Not even the Spanish in the old days took *everything* from their subjects. We are peaceful villagers, señor. We have tried to meet Bocanegro's demands. But no matter how much we give him, he always asks for more. Now we have nothing left to give him. He even has the silver from my poor church. We are desperate. That is why we sent runners for help. Even *los rurales* would be an improvement over Bocanegro and his ruffians."

Captain Gringo glanced at Gaston, who said, "*Oui,* it is an old familiar tale. Are there no local *rurales*, padre?"

"There used to be some police here. Bocanegro's men shot them all. Some they killed in battle. Those who surrendered were shot against a wall, and we were forced to bury them. We have no guns. We have nobody to defend us. Bocanegro has given us twelve hours to raise another tax payment. That is what he calls the money he takes from us—tax payments. He says if we do not have *mucho dinero* for him by dawn, he intends to make an example of us. He made an example of a village up the railroad tracks a week ago. The men were killed, the women were ravaged and *then* killed. They even shot the dogs and pigs. Then they burned the village to the ground."

Captain Gringo said, "Sweet guys. Do you know where your liberator hides out between raids, padre?"

"Hides out? He does not hide out, señor. Bocanegro holds court on a plantation he seized in the interior. He and his *ladrónes* have seized the railroad trains as well. They move *muy* pronto up and down the line, collecting tribute and selecting pretty women from those who do not oppose them, and butchering anyone who does."

Gaston switched to English as he murmured, "Take it easy, Dick. I know that look in your eye. But it's not our fight. We came here to get a boat to Belize, remember?"

Captain Gringo nodded, glancing down the quay at the few masts in sight.

Then Tio Pepe stood up and said, "By the breasts of the Virgin, I am with you, countrymen! We have guns and explosives. This big Yanqui is the famous Captain Gringo! Viva Mexico! Let Bocanegro come! We shall show him how men should fight!"

Another Mexican in the crowd from town gasped and said, "I have heard of the great Captain Gringo! He is said to fight for the *pobrecitos!* We are saved!"

Someone else yelled, "Viva Captain Gringo! Show us how to fight, and our grandchildren will sing songs about you!"

Captain Gringo muttered, "Oh, shit," and Gaston said, "Let it go, Dick. *Sacre* God damn, not only is it not our problem, but if those runners got through *federale* troops should be arriving any minute, and I promise you they won't sing your praises!"

Bubbly blond Phoebe said, "Gee, we can't just leave

these poor people at the mercy of bandits. It wouldn't be British!" and Flora nodded in agreement.

But swishy Chadwick stamped his foot and snapped, "Nonsense! We've no orders to muck about in Mexican affairs!"

That did it.

Captain Gringo sighed and climbed up on the dynamite box so everyone could hear as he announced, "All right. The first thing everyone has to understand is that if I take command, I don't mess around. When I yell froggy, I expect everyone to hop! If we screw up, Bocanegro will give you just what screw-ups deserve. Anyone who disobeys a direct order from me or the leaders I appoint won't die against a wall. He'll die on the spot. If this is getting too rich for anyone's blood, he'd better speak up now or forever hold his peace. If I lead you, I lead you right. If you can't accept me as absolute boss, we'll just be on our way and say no more about it!"

He waited until they shouted a lot among themselves. Then the alcalde held up his hand for silence and said, "We are with you to a man, Captain Gringo. What are your first orders?"

"Generale" Bocanegro was feeling good as he rode toward Vigia Chica in the cool morning trades aboard the last flatcar of his six-car train. He was relaxed and rested after plenty of sleep between two frightened peon girls who'd done to the letter everything he'd demanded. A hero needed to reserve his strength, so it didn't matter if a recently widowed pretty woman and her virgin daughter wept as they serviced one, just so they did all the work. Bocanegro had eaten a good breakfast, prepared by another weeping woman, whom he hadn't gotten around

to ravaging yet. He relaxed in the gilt chair looted from a wealthy planter as he smoked a Havana Perfecto and admired the shine on his booted toes. It was surprising how well a proud hidalgo planter could shine boots with a gun pointed at him, no?

Bocanegro was a big man for this part of Mexico. He couldn't read or write. His mother had been a waterfront whore and his father had been some sailor passing through. But Bocanegro didn't worry about being an ignorant bastard. He'd learned as a boy that when you hit people who are smaller than you, they tended to cry and let you have your way. By the time he'd killed his first man at the age of eleven, Bocanegro had learned that it's even easier to bully people if one has a weapon in one's hands.

The followers riding the train with him were men of similar background and views. There were close to a hundred of them in Bocanegro's strike force. Their *adelitas* and other women captured along the way had been left behind at headquarters. Bocanegro considered himself a military genius who did things right. He was looking forward to the coming fray. He knew the people in the little seaport had no way of meeting his tribute demands. He'd already squeezed the lemon dry. Now he meant to chew up the rind. There would still be a little loot and many pretty girls to be taken. But, mostly, it would be fun. Men who didn't have the balls to butcher human beings just didn't know the sport they were missing. What was a hunt or a bull fight to a man who'd seen human blood spill, eh?

A burly lieutenant made his way back to Bocanegro, saluted, and said, "We are almost there, my *generale*. Do you wish to take command up front?"

Bocanegro took a drag on his fine smoke and said, "It is not important. I do not wish to get locomotive soot on my new linen shirt. You know the plan, Hernan. When we pull into the dockside terminal, you *muchachos* fan out and cover everyone. I will be facing the main plaza as I stand on this flatcar. Naturally, the *pobrecitos* will approach hat in hand to tell me they have no presents for us. Naturally, I will be very cross with them. I shall shoot the alcalde and the priest, as usual. That will be the signal for a general slaughter. Make sure you don't shoot any of the better looking women if it can be avoided, eh?"

Hernan nodded, saluted again, and made his way forward. He didn't relay any messages to the armed desperados he passed aboard the other cars. They all knew what to do.

Hernan climbed over the wood-filled tender and joined the outlaws driving the engine. They were already slowing down. The outskirts of Vigia Chico were just ahead. But what was this? A big tree was down across the tracks!

The man at the throttle swore and said, "That storm must have uprooted that old bastard, dammit!"

As the engineer hit the brakes, Hernan leaned out the side, frowning. If those stupid peasants thought they could save themselves by placing a barricade across the tracks, they were *really* going to get it now!

Hernan said, "Look! That tree never fell. It was chopped down! Stop while we settle accounts with the bastards!"

The locomotive ground to a halt, its cowcatcher fifty feet from the tree across the tracks. But Hernan didn't get to settle much. Captain Gringo opened up with his Maxim from behind said tree, raking the train with hot lead as others with him opened up with small arms!

Hernan gasped and said, "Throw her in reverse!" just before a slug blew him off the side of the locomotive, screaming, gut shot. Another machine-gun round smashed into the engineer's forehead, spattering the fireman with blood and brains. The fireman reversed the gears and opened the throttle wide. Then a bullet went in one ear and out the other, leaving nobody at the controls as the *ladrón* train backed off, picking up speed with every thrust of its drivers.

Aboard, all was chaos. Men lay dead and dying aboard all six flatcars. Others hugged the deck, gibbering with fear. One of them was Bocanegro. What had gone wrong? What could have gone wrong? That had been a *machine gun* back there! Had *federales* been sent to clean him out?

Bocanegro gingerly raised his head as the train moved backward faster and the sounds of gunfire faded away in the distance. From the spacing of those last shots, Bocanegro knew someone was picking off the few men on his side who'd jumped or fallen from the train back there. That was not his problem. His problem was to save himself and the hell with everyone else!

He began to recover his poise as he considered his options. Things could be worse. No matter how many *federale* troops had landed, they could hardly have a railroad train. This one was making good time. It was going much faster than any mounted *federale* could possibly hope to ride. So, he'd have a couple of hours on them when he got back to his own headquarters.

After that, of course, he and his *muchachos* could simply rid themselves of their prisoners, load up the mules, and escape back into the lowland countryside, which they knew so much better than did those sissies from Mexico City.

He rose and surveyed the passing scenery with one hand in his shirt like Napoleon. He knew where he was and felt he had control of his destiny once more. They were backing toward a trestle over a barranca cut by running water through the limestone. When they crossed it, they would stop and destroy the bridge behind them. The natural moat was infested with alligators. Maneaters. Bocanegro had tested this by tossing a screaming captive girl down the barranca walls after she'd acted silly about a little fun.

But where was Hernan? The damned train was going too fast. The outlaw leader kicked a man sprawled at his feet and said, "Go tell them in the engine that I wish to stop on the other side of the bridge."

"Por favor, Bocanegro. I am wounded."

"I spit in your wounds and your mother's milk! Do as I say, you whimpering cur!"

The wounded man drew himself to his hands and knees, sobbing and started to crawl. Bocanegro watched the track ahead. He swore. They were coming to the trestle and moving fast. Perhaps he should reconsider?

Bocanegro shrugged. At this rate they would be back at headquarters in a few minutes. So screw it. By the time *los federales* crossed the trestle, he and his men would be long gone, leaving nothing behind but a burning plantation and dead bodies to bury.

The train rolled out across the trestle. As it got to the middle, Gaston pushed the plunger to detonate the dynamite he and his guides had spent a good part of the night placing under the timber trestle. The dynamite went off with a thunderous roar, lifting trestle and train and then dropping the wreckage and screaming *ladrónes* into the sluggish deep waters below!

Some of the *ladrónes* were killed outright by the explosion. Others died as timbers or rolling stock crushed them like beetles against the muddy bottom of the barranca. Others, stunned, lived a few moments longer. One of them was Bocanegro himself. As the murderous bully fought his way to the surface, ears ringing and coughing muddy water from his windpipe, he glanced wildly around, saw little but blue smoke and utter chaos, and started swimming as bullets spanged the water all around. Tio Pepe, up on the bank, spotted Bocanegro and raised his rifle. Gaston stopped him, saying, *"Merde alors,* don't be so hasty. It's not as if you owed the *chameau* a favor, *hein?"*

"But, Señor Gaston, what if he gets away?"

"He won't. Regard what is swimming to meet him."

Bocanegro saw the alligator, too. He gibbered in terror and tried to get away by swimming to the sheer limestone wall and clambering up out of the water. But the limestone was slimy and offered no handholds. Bocanegro was still clawing at it, tearing his fingernails out by the roots, when the gator lazily opened its jaws and began to munch him for breakfast, a bite at a time.

Other gators were doing the same favors for other screaming *ladrónes* down there. So, Gaston said, "Let us go, my friends. This is no longer amusing. We have a long hike back to town, and our Captain Gringo will no doubt have something better for us to do than feeding animals, *hein?*"

One of the Mexicans from town laughed and said, "I'd say we fed the animals very nicely, thanks to you and Captain Gringo. God knows how we'll ever thank you."

Gaston said, "Don't worry. We'll think of something."

Naturally, the reward Captain Gringo expected from the people of Vigia Chica was safe passage south for all but his Mexican friends, Tio Pepe and his girls. Veronica said she wanted to go with him to be his *adelita* forever. But he told her not to be silly.

The alcalde and his friends agreed to furnish the party a seaworthy vessel and added that they saw no reason to concern their central government with certain details. But the seaworthy part was a little tricky.

There were a few beat-up fishing boats left. Most of the townsmen who'd had decent vessels had loaded aboard their kith and kin and lit out for safer parts when Bocanegro and his thugs first appeared in the neighborhood. Captain Gringo and Gaston inspected what was left. What was left was awful. They were over two hundred sea miles from Belize, and most of that would be open-sea miles. If they stayed much longer, they could be in even more trouble. So, Captain Gringo chose the biggest open trawler he could find and had it hauled out for repairs and refitting. The local ship's carpenters, none of them builders, said they could probably finish the job in twelve hours if they got right to work. So, Captain Gringo asked them to get cracking and offered to pay for the pulque.

Inspired, they agreed to work through *la siesta*. They were grateful indeed. But as the sun rose higher, Captain Gringo and his companions had no reason to be fried alive. So, they ajourned to the nearest waterfront posada to *siesta* up.

Like most native inns, the posada offered spartan accommodations. Mexican peons were used to sleeping on floor mats. But the coral block walls were thick, and the small individual rooms were cool as well as pretty dark. The tiny windows were covered with jalousie shutters. Captain Gringo hung his duds on a wooden peg, tucked his gun rig between the floor mat and plastered wall, and lay down, nude, with smoking material and a jug of not bad cerveza. He wasn't too surprised when Flora and Phoebe joined him. But he saw they'd brought little Veronica along.

As all three of them proceed to shuck, Phoebe, who seemed to be the ring master, said, "We explained the rules to Veronica and she says it sounds like fun."

He said, "Fun for who? I'm only one guy, gals! Are you sure you know what they're talking about, Veronica?"

The little Mexican girl said, *"Sí.* I would rather say adios to you all by myself. But Señorita Phoebe has been kind enough to explain your gringo customs."

"I'll bet she has. Where's Gaston? I may need reinforcements."

Veronica dropped naked to her knees beside him as

she giggled and said, "Tia Maria and Tia Lolita are saying goodbye to *him*. Tia Juana told them he is *muy toro* and . . ."

"Right, it's Tia Juana's turn with Tio Pepe," Captain Gringo cut in.

Veronica was closest, so he took her in his arms first. But as he kissed her, Flora tapped his naked back and said, "My turn, I believe."

He laughed, said, "Get your own girl," and rolled Veronica on her back to mount her. The blond and brunette English girls got on the mat with them. There was plenty of room. Quarters were nicely tight in Veronica. So, he paid little attention to Phoebe and Flora as he enjoyed the amoral, childlike peon girl. But as he was coming, Veronica laughed and said, "Oh, that looks so silly!"

He followed her gaze, and, yeah, the blonde and brunette were going sixty-nine again. Veronica asked him why and he said, "I told her to get her own girl. Could you, ah, raise your knees a little?"

She could, and it felt hot as hell. The sensuous moans and slurping sounds coming from the other couple were sort of stimulating, too. But when the uncomplicated little Mexican girl came a second time, he faked his own orgasm. He had to husband his resources, and Flora had rolled free of Phoebe and was writhing on the mat as she pleaded, "Do *me*, Dick! I'm so excited I can't stand it!"

He said, "Excuse me," to Veronica and rolled off her to board Flora. As he entered her taller, slimmer, firmer body, he had to admit she had a point. He'd forgotten how great she was. He came so quickly it would have been impolite, had not Flora already been so stimulated by Phoebe's bisexual tongue that she came with him.

He kept going to be polite. He heard Veronica gasp in mingled surprise and pleasure, and, yeah, when he looked, Phoebe's blond head was between the peon girl's brown thighs as she crouched on her knees and elbows, eating her passionately. Her pale derriere and golden-fuzzed slit were aimed right at him. So, he admired the view as he went on making it with Flora. The once-prudish English girl was so aroused by the sheer perversity of the situation that she came repeatedly as he coasted in her. Just as it was starting to become work, Flora rolled her dark head wildly from side to side and gasped as she said, "Enough! Have mercy! I have to take a breather!"

He laughed, withdrew, and crawled up behind Phoebe to mount her from behind. As he entered her blond love gates, he was again delighted by the contrast. As he started humping, he muttered, "That's what I like best about women. Every time you make one, she feels better than anything you've ever had."

Phoebe didn't answer. Her mouth was full. Veronica grinned at him across Phoebe's arched spine and cupped her own brown breasts up to him as she said, "Oh, this is so delicious! I can hardly wait to tell the other girls of my village what we have been missing!"

"Just don't mention it at confession and you ought to be all right."

Veronica laughed and said, "We never tell the padre things like that. The Church says fun like this is forbidden. The Church is *loco en la cabeza,* no?"

The blonde between them arched her spine yet more and began to wag her tail bone like an eager puppy as she expanded and contracted on his questing shaft. She must have been excited at the other end as well, since Veronica had her head back, eyes closed, and was moving her brown body to literally screw Phoebe's face. Phoebe hissed in orgasmic pleasure as she tried to bite Captain Gringo off at the roots with her love maw while shoving her tongue in Veronica's mouth. The results were explosive for all three of them. Phoebe rolled out of the way, gasping, "Coo, I just died and went to heaven!" as the only male

173

in the orgy fell forward atop Veronica, got into Veronica before it could go soft, and sighed as he said, "Here we go round the mulberry bush. Hi, Veronica. Long time no screw."

She laughed and enfolded him in her brown arms and legs. But he just lay there for the moment, getting his breath back as he enjoyed the message of her postclimactic contractions. How could he have forgotten that Veronica had the nicest box?

Flora sat up, frowning in concentration, and said, "I say. We seem to have done all the easy stuff. Why don't we put our heads together and think of something really low? One doesn't have a golden opportunity like this every day, you know."

Phoebe reached for her chum's groin as she suggested, "I've got a better idea where we should all put our heads. Have any of you lot ever heard of a daisy chain?"

Captain Gringo laughed and said, "It won't work. All the daisy chains I ever heard of consist of one sex. I understand they're very popular at all-girl schools."

Phoebe said, "They are indeed. But not to worry, Dick. I'm sure we can fit you in."

He grimaced and said, "I'd better just watch." None of them had noticed that he hadn't been kissing anybody lately. All four of them could have used a bath, and the three girls, while still serviceable for his old organ grinder, were a mite gamy.

So he leaned against the wall and watched, bemused, as the three of them formed a head-to-pussy triangle, with Flora eating Veronica, for a change, Veronica taking care of Phoebe's blond crotch, while Phoebe did the same for Flora. He was a little disgusted at first. The room smelled musky and the girls were really acting nuts. But as they heated up again, he started to rise to the occasion again. He didn't want to get into that, but he sure intended to take care of the first dropout.

It was a shame, in a way, that they'd be leaving Veronica behind here. On the other hand, maybe it was just as well. Who had the strength to cope with three dedicated nymphomaniacs?

By that evening the lug-rigged fishing boat was in as good a shape as it was going to get. So, Captain Gringo and his friends started stowing things aboard. Tio Pepe and his harem had already headed for home, saving tearful farewells. Veronica had left walking kind of funny. But nobody noticed. The two tias who'd said a proper adios to Gaston were walking the same way. Come to think of it, everybody was. He could see by the way young Chadwick was mincing that he, too, had been well laid that afternoon. Captain Gringo, Gaston, and Clarke just looked tired.

They had their gear on board and were saying adios to the alcalde and other important villagers when a shout rang out and they saw some men in the ominous uniform of *los rurales* headed their way along the quay!

Captain Gringo snapped, "All aboard, gang! I'll shove off!"

The alcalde said, "Oh, our call for help must have gotten through after all!"

"Now you tell us!" sighed the tall American as his companions threw themselves aboard the boat while he unfastened the lines and followed. Gaston already had the sail up, close-hauled to move them with the trades almost abeam.

The little boat began to move as the townspepole got out of the way of the *rurale* charge. *Los rurales* weren't kidding around. They had their guns out, and the leader demanded, "Halt! Who are you and what are you doing here on Mexican soil?"

It seemed a reasonable question. But nobody answered. There wasn't a thing they could say that would please the Mexican police!

The leader shouted, "I am warning you!" and, as the boat moved even farther away, he barked a command to his men and they lined up to form a no-kidding firing squad. They didn't fire. Captain Gringo rose amidships with the Maxim braced on one hip, said, "Okay, you asked who I am," and chopped them down like a row of cornstalks.

By this time they were making for the harbor bar at a nice clip, so he put down the Maxim. Gaston, at the helm, said, *"Eh bien,* we won't be able to go back there again, but who'd want to, *hein?"*

Chadwick said, "You shouldn't have killed them!" But even his lover, Clarke, thought that was so dumb he growled, "Shut up, you silly sod. What were we supposed to do, suck them off?"

"Don't be nasty. This could cause an international incident."

Gaston laughed and said, *"Mes non, mes amies,* Dick is already an international incident. Your Greystoke knew that when he hired us."

They steered for the open sea and made it. As the moon came out, they saw that nobody was following them. The sea was calm and laced with green fire. The trades were fresh and steady. They were making a good six knots. By dawn they'd be . . . still in Mexican waters, damm it!

They made it. It wasn't easy and it took forever, but, by hugging the coast and sheltering in the mangroves by day and sailing at night, they finally limped into Belize. Their beat-up little fishing boat wasn't any more interesting to the British customs people than it might have been to any patrol or pirate craft who'd spotted its tiny tattered sail on the way south. So, nobody bothered the wilted travelers as they spotted *La Nombre Nada* moored next to Greystoke's yacht and sailed over to join them.

The girls headed right for the showers after Greystoke

welcomed them aboard. The two mariposas saw they weren't needed, and Clarke took Chadwick to wash the sea salt and grime from his tender behind, too. As they left, Gaston was the only one crude enough to pass a remark about dropping the soap. Captain Gringo and Gaston had the answers Greystoke wanted to hear, and, what the hell, they were used to being grungy. So, they all cooled off in Greystoke's salon, enjoying the shade and some decent booze for a change. Greystoke brought them up-to-date first, as they'd been the ones lost to human ken the past few days. As they could see, *Nombre Nada* had made it through the storm. When the British crew had gone back to pick up Captain Gringo and the others, Sir Basil Hakim had put a burst of 20 mm across their bows. So, they'd assumed the worse and reported back to Belize. Greystoke said he'd keep *Nombre Nada* where it was and swap it back with Esperanza the next time she was up this way, if she made it.

Captain Gringo told Greystoke everything they'd been through, except for the sexy parts. Greystoke frowned when he heard about the deal they'd made with Hakim. But before he could say anything, Captain Gringo explained, "Look, the little shit was going to take us out and tap that line in any case, whether we made a deal or not. I sold him worthless info and a dead cable for our lives. I thought you'd be pleased that for once I brought almost everybody back alive."

Greystoke sighed and said, "Well, that is a switch. I suppose it was hoping too much for you to have liquidated Hakim and his lot."

"Hey, *you* liquidate him if that's what Whitehall wants! Aside from his being a dangerous little prick, Gaston and I are soldiers of fortune, not paid assassins."

Gaston blew a thoughtful smoke ring and chimed in, "I will murder someone on occasion if the money is interesting. But it has just occurred to me, M'sieur Greystoke, that you might have been trying to buy a killing *très* cheap!"

Greystoke looked innocent. Gaston grimaced, waved his cigar at Captain Gringo, and explained, "You knew my excitable youth, here, is inclined to be destructive. Hakim has too many friends in high British places for you to order any British agent, officially, to put Woodbine Arms, Limited, out of business. On the other hand, you issued two machine guns and a crate of high explosives to this adorable child, knowing full well Sir Basil might be paying us a social call!"

Greystoke said, "Don't be ridiculous. Hakim is a thorn in our side, but he is on our side, more than Krupp of Essen."

"Eh bien, and does not Sir Basil have stock in Krupp as well as the British Woodbine industrial complex?"

"Look, that fucking little Turk has his finger in every pie. But forget about him now. Since Hakim's yacht arrived here this morning, just ahead of you, he obviously didn't learn anything damaging to the Crown. He wouldn't have abandoned that cable so soon if it weren't still dead. Your mission was to spy on the Spanish. I must say I'm a bit disappointed in the meager results."

Captain Gringo took another sip of gin and tonic and said, "Bullshit. Our mission was to guard your sneaks, and we did it pretty good. We weren't ordered to find out anything about the Cuban situation. If Boggs and Carmichael hadn't been killed, I wouldn't know as much as I do."

"Agreed. But, dash it all, how much do you really know?"

"We told you. Apparently somebody's in the market for a mess of armor plate and they think they can get it cheaper from John Brown, Limited, than Hakim's rolling mills in Blighty. Frankly, I don't see what difference this could mean to Whitehall, since the business figures to be all in the family. The queen doesn't stop any lime juicer from selling anything from a pop gun to a battleship to anyone with money, does she?"

"Of course not. England is the Workshop of the World. But we do like to keep track of such purchases."

"Yeah. Someday you'll look pretty silly when a British gunboat sinks a British gunboat, huh?"

Greystoke sniffed and said, "I hardly think it's the place of a soldier of fortune to make such moral judgments. Let's stick to the point. We've established that someone in Cuba is shopping for armor plate. What do you suppose that means?"

Captain Gringo shrugged and said, "Don't look at me! How the fuck should I know?"

Gaston said, "It makes no sense either way. The Cuban guerrillas would hardly have need for armor plate, since they have no navy, unless the U.S. decides to supply them with one. In which case they still would not be shopping for armor plate."

Greystoke nodded and said, "The Spanish must be beefing up their fleet, then. There's a Royal Spanish navy yard in Santiago."

Gaston shook his head and said, *"Mes non.* You children forget I have been in this business some time. So, I am *très* familiar with Spanish military policy. Spain operates on *les* cheaps. Their army marches in rope-soled sandals. Their navy is held together by rust and Spanish macho. The old conquistadores were fighting sonsofthe-bitch. But their great-grandchildren have gone to seed resting on their ancestors' reputation. One imagines the future shall see a similar softening of British resolve. But whether your grandchildren regard the British flag waving from Pine to Palm or not is beside the point. The Spanish Colonial Empire is *très finis.* Spain is not going to spend enough money on new arms to matter. They're having enough trouble meeting the payroll of their pathetic army and navy as it is. Besides, they don't have time to began a new navy."

Greystoke frowned and stared down at his empty glass as he mused aloud, *"Somebody* seems to be in the market for a lot of armor plate. Hello, I need another drink."

He reached for a pull cord to summon help. The beautiful Indira came in, wearing a see-through sari and carrying another round of drinks on a tray. As she handed Captain Gringo another gin and tonic, he examined her nipples and said, "Oh, right, a double agent. I should have known."

Greystoke smiled fondly after the Hindu girl's receding derriere as he said, "Of course, Hakim sent her back to spy on me some more as soon as they got back. But she knows which side her bread is buttered on."

"Yeah. I'm sure you guys have a lot of fans in India. Listen, Greystoke, we're talking in circles and it's getting late. Fuck the Intelligence data and let's talk sense. Gaston and I had a deal with you. We carried out our part of the bargain, and we want to get back to Costa Rica and unwind. When do we get paid?"

Greystoke nodded, reached in his jacket, and took out a roll of bills. He counted out a modest sheaf and handed them to Captain Gringo. The tall American counted, frowned, and growled, "You call this money? I don't!"

Greystoke said, "I'm afraid it's the best I can do, chaps. You did trade a modern, expensive yacht for that wonky native schooner, you know."

"Bullshit. *Nombre Nada* isn't that beat-up, and besides, you'll be able to swap back with Esperanza in time."

"Whitehall's accountants don't deal in futures, Dick. They were very cross with me when I last communicated with them. Besides, you know I only hired you two unofficially. Whitehall doesn't pay officer's wages to, ah, I'm afraid they called you beachcombers."

Captain Gringo's eyes narrowed dangerously as he rose to his feet and spat, "You cheating sonofabitch!"

Gaston stood up, grabbed his arm, and warned, "Take the money and run, Dick! I'd like to hit him, too, but let us be *pratique, hein?*"

Greystoke remained at ease as he smiled up at them and said, "He's right, you know. You two still depend on my continued goodwill if you mean to leave this British colony unmolested."

Captain Gringo snarled, "I'll molest you, you welshing motherfucker!"

But Gaston put his back into dragging him toward the door as he insisted, *"Mes non,* listen to me. I have the better answer. Trust me."

Captain Gringo knew that look in Gaston's eye. So, he nodded and said, "Okay, Greystoke. Half a loaf is better than none, but you're still a sonofabitch and I hope the kaiser wins in a couple of years."

Greystoke smiled thinly and replied, "I'm sure we can keep him at bay at least twenty. *Vaya con Dios,* chaps."

Captain Gringo waited until they were safely ashore before he turned to Gaston and said, "Okay, spill it. How are we planning to pay that bastard back for double-crossing us again?"

Gaston chuckled and said, "By double-crossing him, of course. First let us check into a hotel, make ourselves presentable, and send Sir Basil a message to meet us on neutral ground, *hein?*"

They started walking into town. But Captain Gringo said, "We don't have anything left to sell him." Then he frowned and added, "Do you think that bit about John Brown, Limited, underbidding him might be worth anything to the old goat? It's the only thing he might not know about the deal."

Gaston shook his head and said, "He's heard that

already. He would not have left the cable tap so soon if it had not come back to life shortly after we abandoned it to him, *non?*"

"Shit, you're right. By now Hakim knows as much as Greystoke, and it's still not saying much. How much could he want to pay us just for verifying what he already knows?"

"I think it ought to be worth at least a couple of thousand, Dick. I shall explain it to you both when we put our heads together, *hein?* It is rather complicated, and I so enjoy surprises."

Captain Gringo and Gaston were lounging in the hotel tap room, clean-shaven and wearing fresh linen suits, when Sir Basil and two bodyguards arrived. They were dressed spiffy, too.

The Merchant of Death took a seat across the table from the soldiers of fortune. His bodyguards covered the doorways casually while their boss talked. Sir Basil said, "I came as soon as I got your message, chaps. You say you have something for me?"

Gaston said, "*Mes oui*. First, I would like a thousand dollars for my young friend here. Then I would like another thousand in my own hot little hand."

"I don't buy pigs in a poke, Gaston."

"You have no choice. I find it *très fatigue* to deal with people who beat down the price once they have what they want from us. We did the job British Intelligence hired us to do. We were paid off in *les* peanuts. Do you grasp my point?"

Hakim chuckled and said, "British Intelligence has to be thrifty. They're spread so thin. Do I have your word as a fellow scoundrel that you have two thousand dollars' worth of whatever for me?"

"You do. It is worth considerably more. But we are in a hurry. Dick and I were not the only people Greystoke was out to diddle. You were shafted up the derriere, too."

Hakim raised an eyebrow, counted out the money, and handed it to Gaston, saying, "Keep talking."

Gaston said, "Greystoke knew from the beginning that you were keeping tabs on him. You deal in arms. British Intelligence keeps track of everyone who buys them, true?"

"That's not worth two thousand dollars, Gaston."

"I am merely setting the stage for the bedroom farce we've all been playing, with Greystoke writing the script. He went to great pains to let you know he was sending a *très dramatique* spy mission to listen in on a mysterious, uncharted undersea cable, knowing you would follow us to see what on earth or under the sea was going on."

Hakim frowned and asked, "Are you saying you two and those British agents you led were all duped?"

"Why not? It's true. As Dick, here, pointed out at once, Butcher Weyler has no reason to communicate secretly with *el Presidente* Diaz. They are both dedicated sonsofthebitch. But Weyler is a Dutch-Spanish Grandee, and Diaz is a Mestizo who hates the breed from his bones out. Diaz would not lift a finger to help Spain. Moreover, he owes his long reign of terror to the fact that he kisses Washington's ass every time it does not get in the way of his other unpleasant habits, *non?*"

Hakim nodded and said, "Very well, who did lay that cable from Cuba to the mainland, the Cuban rebels?"

"*Mes non.* How could they? Indeed, how could anybody lay a cable from Cuba to the mainland without the Spanish or Mexican authorities being aware of it and asking questions about it? That cable does not run from Mexico to Cuba. It is simply a few miles of stage setting, running from a secret British base in the Yucatán jungles to deep water, where, most naturally, nobody would dive for it."

Both Hakim and Captain Gringo started in astonishment at Gaston. Captain Gringo caught on first. He nodded and said, "Right. That accounts for a lot of things. The cable went dead when the agents on shore moved back from the hurricane waters that night. They'd already fed us the bullshit Greystoke told them to. When they spotted Hakim's yacht in the channel, they started sending the same fake messages again."

Hakim was sharp. But not that sharp. He said, "It makes no sense! Why on earth would Greystoke have one set of British agents spying on another set of British agents?"

Captain Gringo said, "I can answer that. I was wondering why the bunch he sent with us were so half-ass. British Intelligence is supposed to be good. He saddled me with in inept skipper, a couple of swishes, and two nice little dames who, while they were nice indeed, were probably little more than secretaries back in Whitehall. I had to keep explaining things any trained spy would know. Greystoke's *sharp* agents were hiding out on shore, sending garbage out to the end of a cable going nowhere. The end must be sealed and the circuit's looped inside the sheathing, see?"

"Never mind the bloody electricity! Why did they do it?"

Gaston said, "To screw *you,* of course. Greystoke knew you would want to know what was being sent. Knowing you, he knew you would either get what you were after, or perhaps be liquidated by us, which would suit Greystoke just as well. After we left, you did pick up that business about John Brown, Limited, offering a better buy on armor plate than your own Woodbine industries, *non?*"

"Of course, I must say it gave me a bit of a turn. I thought I was already undercutting John Brown on armor plate."

"You probably are. You use inferior steel and don't pay

those Oriental workers you sneak into England as much as John Brown, Limited, has to pay its English workers."

"Let's not be sarky. We were discussing those wonky messages to nowhere."

"*Merde alors,* you still don't see it? Greystoke's planted misinformation was not meant for the fishes. It was meant for *you!* Thanks to the distressing posturing of Queen Victoria's German grandson, Kaiser Willy, Britain has embarked on a furious ship-building program, *non?* To build a lot of new dreadnaughts in a hurry, one needs to buy a lot of expensive armor plate. Do I have to lead you to the blackboard by the hand?"

Hakim blanched and gasped as he said, "Of course! The sonsofbitches are trying to beat me down on the price of my rolled steel! I see it all now! I *was* about to cable my agents in London to quote new prices undercutting John Brown and Armstrong!"

"*Oui,* and the Royal Navy would have thanked British Intelligence very much. It is my guess they are also trying to lower the price of armor plate from other suppliers by letting them, ah, discover for themselves that your Woodbine plate can be had at most reasonable prices, *hein?*"

Sir Basil gravely took out his wallet and emptied it on the table, saying, "This is all I brought with me. I seldom tip generously, but you chaps have just saved me from making a ghastly mistake."

As Gaston divided the extra six hundred with Captain Gringo, Sir Basil added, "You say they also hoped we'd wind up killing one another?"

Gaston said, "That would have been icing on the cake. One gathers M'sieur Greystoke is *très* jealous of your relationship with Prince Edward. If you managed to get yourself killed before the next important war, your surviving board of directors may be less *fatigue* to deal with. Meanwhile, since he can't really order you assassinated, Greystoke intended to keep you as confused as possible.

Now that you know all, one gathers Her Majesty will not be getting any battleships at bargain-basement prices in the near future."

"That I can promise you! I'd like to stay and chat some more, chaps. But I really must be getting to the nearest cable office!"

The gnomish Turk or whatever left with his bodyguards in tow, moving fast for a man with such short legs. Gaston leaned back and said, "How did you like that performance, Dick?"

"It more than made up the difference Greystoke cheated us out of. Are you saying it was all bullshit?"

"*Mes non*, it might have been true, for all we know. In any case, it fit together, and the Byzantine chess game those two are playing is no longer of concern to us. I have a few rogues to look up here in Belize, if we are to book safe passage to Costa Rica and a well-earned rest. What are your plans for this evening, Dick? Are you going to look up those English girls or see what you can pick up in the sunset *paseo?*"

Captain Gringo grinned and said, "I'm looking forward to a good book to read, alone, on clean sheets in a good hotel, with nobody shooting at me for a while. I'm afraid the girls and I exhausted all the possible ways to come, and I don't want to get mixed up with any locals before we leave."

Gaston nodded, finished his drink, and said they'd talk about plans when he got back in the wee small hours, the exact time depending on whether he met any rogue in a skirt or not.

Captain Gringo enjoyed an early supper and went out to sit on the hotel veranda to watch the sun go down. The *paseo* would be starting any minute now. He knew that at least a couple of the girls strolling the plaza would be pretty and more than willing. But he told his genital region to hang loose. He was beginning to come back to life down there again. They hadn't been able to play slap and tickle coming down the coast in the crowded boat. But he was in the clear, for once, and he knew how hard it was for a big blond Anglo to stay out of trouble picking up local talent in the plaza of an evening down here.

He sat there until a mosquito bit him. Then he rose, went inside, and stocked up on smoking and reading material at the lobby newsstand. The high yellow girl behind the counter had a nice smile. Her tits weren't bad, either. But she worked too close to home, so he just paid for his cigars and magazines and left her to Fate.

He went upstairs. Like the poet said, in the tropics the dawn comes up like thunder and the sunsets don't mess around either. It was already getting dark. They hadn't switched on the hall lights yet. So, he was able to spot the sliver of electric light under the door of his private room before he got close enough to matter.

He frowned, looked around, saw that the hallway was deserted, and drew his .38 before tucking the cigar box and magazines under his other elbow and gingerly trying the knob.

The door wasn't locked. He opened it and moved in fast, sliding his back along the wall beside the door as he slammed it shut after him while covering the figure on his bed.

Then he lowered the muzzle of his pistol as he saw that she wasn't carrying any concealed weapons. Indira, the tawny Hindu girl from Greystoke's yacht, was reclining atop the bed covers stark naked. Her sari was neatly folded over the end of the bed and her only concession to modesty was the caste mark on her forehead, above her big, dark smoldering eyes. Her long black hair failed to cover her chocolate-drop nipples and her legs weren't coyly crossed. She had her long taffy legs relaxed and parted enough to let him see that she was a brunette all over.

He nodded, took off his new hat and jacket, and hung them up as he asked conversationally, "Who sent you to spy on me, Hakim or Greystoke?"

Indira's voice was as matter-of-fact as she replied, "It was my own idea."

"Oh? You can't be hard up, considering how you've been passed around."

She grimaced and said, "Yes and no. I overheard those English girls discussing your skills as they were, ah, soaping each other in the shower. But you're right about my being passed around, and I'm bloody sick of it. They say you and the Frenchman are going to Costa Rica, where things are calm and the living is easy. I want you to take me with you, Dick. I have a little money saved up. But I'm afraid I only have one thing I can offer you for my passage."

"Don't sweat it. It looks like a nice little passage indeed."

So, she lay back calmly, eyes half-closed and inscrutable as she watched him undress. He got down to his pants. Then he moved over, sat on the edge of the bed, and said, "Look, honey. I don't shoot fish in a barrel. If Gaston works out a no-sweat, no-questions deal, you can come along. No strings. You don't have to put out if you don't feel like it."

Her luminous ebony eyes widened as she stared up at him and said, "I think you really mean that. But now that we're both undressed, well, don't you think I'm as pretty as those silly English girls?"

He said, "Prettier," as he slipped out of his pants, took her in his arms, and slipped into her as their lips met in a smoldering kiss. It was no bigger a lie than the bullshit she was handing him. He knew Greystoke had probably sent her to find out what he and Hakim had been talking about when some other damned British spy tailed Hakim from his yacht. But, no problem, he'd think up something innocent for her to report when she "changed her mind" about going to Costa Rica with him after all. Meanwhile, she was giving one hell of a performance, and the odds were he'd never have made out this good at the *paseo* tonight.

DIRTY HARRY by Dane Hartman
Never before published or seen on screen.

He's "Dirty Harry" Callahan—tough, unorthodox, no-nonsense plain-clothesman extraordinaire of the San Francisco Police Department...Inspector #71 assigned to the bruising, thankless homicide detail...A consummate crimebuster nothing can stop—not even the law! Explosive mysteries involving racketeers, murderers, extortionists, pushers, and skyjackers: savage, bizarre murders, accomplished with such cunning and expertise that the frustrated S.F.P.D. finds itself without a single clue; hair-raising action and violence as Dirty Harry arrives on the scene, armed with nothing but a Smith & Wesson .44 and a bag of dirty tricks; unbearable suspense and hairy chase sequences as Dirty Harry sleuths to unmask the villain and solve the mystery. Dirty Harry—when the chips are down, he's the most low-down cop on the case.

5 EXCITING ADVENTURE SERIES
MEN OF ACTION BOOKS

THE BEST OF ADVENTURE
by RAMSAY THORNE

__RENEGADE #1		(C90-976, $1.95)
__RENEGADE #3	FEAR MERCHANT	(C90-761, $1.95)
__RENEGADE #4	DEATH HUNTER	(C90-902, $1.95)
__RENEGADE #5	MACUMBA KILLER	(C90-234, $1.95)
__RENEGADE #6	PANAMA GUNNER	(C90-235, $1.95)
__RENEGADE #7	DEATH IN HIGH PLACES	(C90-548, $1.95)
__RENEGADE #9	HELL RAIDER	(C90-550, $1.95)
__RENEGADE #10	THE GREAT GAME	(C90-737, $1.95)
__RENEGADE #11	CITADEL OF DEATH	(C90-738, $1.95)
__RENEGADE #12	THE BADLANDS BRIGADE	(C90-739, $1.95)
__RENEGADE #13	THE MAHOGANY PIRATES	(C30-123, $1.95)
__RENEGADE #14	HARVEST OF DEATH	(C30-124, $1.95)
__RENEGADE #15	TERROR TRIAL	(C30-125, $1.95)

To order, use the coupon below. If you prefer to use your own stationery, please include complete title as well as book number and price. Allow 4 weeks for delivery.

WARNER BOOKS
P.O. Box 690
New York, N.Y. 10019

Please send me the books I have checked. I enclose a check or money order (not cash), plus 50¢ per order and 50¢ per copy to cover postage and handling.*

_____ Please send me your free mail order catalog. (If ordering only the catalog, include a large self-addressed, stamped envelope.)

Name _____

Address _____

City _____

State _____ Zip _____

*N.Y. State and California residents add applicable sales tax